**Other Books in the Keystone Stables Series**

# Blue Ribbon Champ

BOOK 6

### KEYSTONE
### Stables

Formerly Titled *Skye's Final Test*

..... *Marsha Hubler* .....

ZONDERVAN.com/
AUTHORTRACKER
follow your favorite authors

We want to hear from you. Please send your comments about this book to us in care of zreview@zondervan.com. Thank you.

Zonderkidz

*Blue Ribbon Champ*
Formerly titled *Skye's Final Test*
Copyright © 2005, 2009 by Marsha Hubler

Requests for information should be addressed to:
Zonderkidz, *Grand Rapids, MI 49530*

---

Library of Congress Cataloging-in-Publication Data

Hubler, Marsha, 1947-
   [Skye's final test]
   Blue ribbon Champ / by Marsha Hubler.
      p. cm. — (Keystone Stables ; bk. 6)
   Summary: One of the special-needs children riding horses at Keystone Stables during the summer has Down syndrome and when his affection for Skye embarrasses her, she begins to treat him harshly.
   ISBN 978-0-310-71797-3 (softcover : alk. paper)
   [1. Foster home care—Fiction. 2. Down syndrome—Fiction. 3. People with mental disabilities—Fiction. 4. Horses—Fiction. 5. Christian life—Fiction.]
I. Title.
   PZ7.H86325Bl 2010
   [Fic]—dc22                                     2009013981

---

*Interior illustrator: Lyn Boyer*
*Interior design and composition: Carlos Estrada and Sherri L. Hoffman*

*Printed in the United States of America*

---

13 14 15 16 • 24 23 22 21 20 19 18 17 16 15 14 13 12 11 10 9 8 7 6 5 4

*To Patti Souder
and the Montrose Christian Writers Conference staff
who brought my ideas for this series and
Zonderkidz together on the same page.*

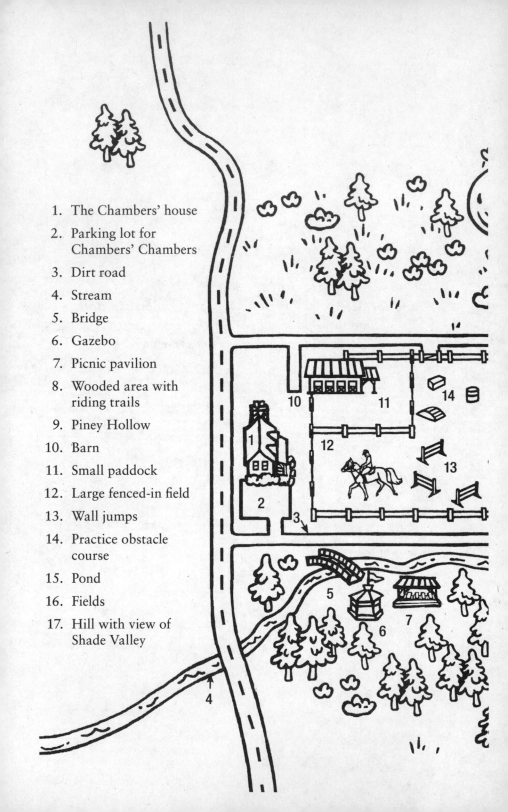

1. The Chambers' house
2. Parking lot for Chambers' Chambers
3. Dirt road
4. Stream
5. Bridge
6. Gazebo
7. Picnic pavilion
8. Wooded area with riding trails
9. Piney Hollow
10. Barn
11. Small paddock
12. Large fenced-in field
13. Wall jumps
14. Practice obstacle course
15. Pond
16. Fields
17. Hill with view of Shade Valley

# Map of the Chambers' Ranch

should've gone to Aunt Dot's in Charleston for the summer!" Skye made her point perfectly clear as she shampooed her horse in the Keystone Stables paddock. "I'm really not looking forward to a summer with Joey Klingerman again."

"Well, why didn't you go to Charleston?" Morgan shot back. "I'm sure Champ would've had a simply marvelous time here without you." From her wheelchair, Skye's foster sister busied herself polishing a saddle on a sawhorse just outside the barn door.

Skye threw her arms around Champ's drenched neck and clung to him like a wet rag. "But I can't get along without him, Morgan. Not for a whole summer. I'd just die!"

The sorrel Quarter Horse nickered and nodded as though in agreement with Skye's dramatic words.

Skye kissed Champ on the nose and then sighed as she wiped his neck with a dry cloth. "I know Joey can't help it that he has Down syndrome, but he just won't leave me alone. Mom's been helping me to try and understand, and I found a neat website that explains all about kids like him, but — "

"And, Skye," Morgan teased, flipping back her long red locks, "what about Chad? You'd die without him too, wouldn't you?"

Skye's face flushed red-hot and she giggled. "Cut it out. You know I'm going nowhere but here for the whole summer. Mom and Dad need both of us, I guess. And Chad? Well ... I ..."

"Did I hear my name?" A teenager in a dark brown Stetson, plaid shirt, and jeans led a buckskin horse out of the barn. "What can I do for you ladies?" Brown eyes flashed in Skye's direction.

Although Skye was soaked and fairly cool from Champ's bath, her cheeks flushed hotter than ever. She threw a quick glance at Chad and returned to her hosing job. "Oh—ah—nothing," she stammered. "We're just discussing the summer."

"Yeah," Morgan added, "and all the work that's ahead of us."

"But working with the horses is fun—most of the time." Skye positioned herself so she could eye Chad.

Chad led the buckskin into the paddock, tied him to a fence post, and started to brush his shiny tan coat. "Yeah, even though Mr. C. pays me for helping, it *is* a lot of fun. The money goes into my college fund, and I get to play with horses and kids all summer. Now in my book that's one super job. Are all the summer students here?"

Skye peeked over her horse's withers, watching Chad's every move. "Yeah. All four of them are here, bag and baggage. Sorry to say, Mom and Dad picked up Joey at the bus station right after church."

Leaning over the horse's back, Chad poked back his Stetson, revealing a clump of blond curls. "Joey Klingerman's coming again? Why are you sorry?"

"'Cause I have a slight problem with him, that's all," she said weakly.

"A problem?" Chad asked.

10

Ignoring Chad's question, Skye busied herself with water and bubbles. *Me and my big mouth.*

"Joey bugs her to death!" Morgan put in her two cents' worth.

*Another big mouth!* Skye fumed. Shielding herself behind Champ, she shot a piercing glare at Morgan and shook her head.

A fake Cheshire grin masked Morgan's freckles. *Sorry!* Her lips formed the word as she resumed soaping the saddle.

"Joey bugs you?" Chad boomed right behind Skye.

"Yikes!" Skye squeaked as she jumped to attention like a soldier called to arms.

Chad and Morgan burst out laughing.

Skye faced Chad in mock anger. "Very funny, Chad Dressler."

Chad's twin dimples highlighted his devilish smile. "Sorry. Didn't mean to scare you—much."

"Yeah, right!" Skye said. *But you can scare me anytime!*

Chad picked up a cloth and started drying Champ's head. "Seriously, what's wrong with Joey? He was here last year, and I didn't notice any problem with him. He listened and followed all the rules, as far as I can remember."

*That wasn't the problem!* Skye didn't need to remind herself.

Morgan leaned forward on the padded saddle seat. "Well, problem or not, he's up at the house with the others right now getting the whole nine yards from Mr. and Mrs. C. 'Do this! Don't do that!' The kids probably feel like they're in some kind of prison!"

"It mustn't seem like prison to Joey, or he wouldn't have come back," Chad said.

Skye turned the hose nozzle off and started to dry the back part of Champ. Out of the corner of her eye, she watched Chad's every move.

*Time to change the subject—and fast,* she told herself. "Well, I sure remember how I felt when I first came here as a know-it-all foster kid. I thought a straitjacket would have been better. But it didn't take me long to get used to all the rules."

"Me neither," Morgan said, relaxing into her chair. "The cool stuff about bein' a foster kid here far outweighs the negatories."

"Negatories?" Skye giggled as she slid her fingers through her long brown hair. "Is that a word?"

"Not sure." Morgan giggled too. "But it sounded good."

"I think it's 'negatives'!" Chad finished wiping off the front of Champ. He pulled a hoof pick out of his back pocket, headed to the buckskin, and lifted one of its front legs.

*He is so-o-o smart!* Skye concluded.

"Easy, Bucky," Chad said, carefully examining the triangular pad on the bottom of the horse's hoof. "We've gotta clean your frogs out—and good. Skye," he said in his next breath, "speaking of problems, how'd Bucky's thrush do over the winter?"

"Every once in a while it'd flare up, especially if we didn't keep his stall clean and dry. Dad said once a horse tangles with that nasty infection, he can get it again in a wink."

"Yeah," Morgan said, "I remember when we got him at auction. Auction horses are risky any way you look at it. Even then, he had a real bad case of thrush in that front right hoof."

"And ever since then we've had to keep an eye on it," Skye added.

Skye studied Chad as he cleaned both of the horse's front hooves. "Uh-oh," he said, still bent over with one hoof resting on his knee, "I think we have a touch of it right here on each side of this frog, Skye. Come here and look."

Skye rushed to Chad's side and examined Bucky's hoof. The deep crevices on both sides of the tattered frog were lined with a pitch-black "dirt." As Chad scraped it out, Bucky's hoof gave off a smell that stank worse than last month's garbage.

"Whew," Skye said, "that's thrush all right."

Morgan set her soap and cloth on the saddle seat. "I'll get the bottle of hydrogen peroxide." She motored into the barn.

"In the meantime," Skye said to Chad as she walked back to her own horse, "get some water and scrub that out real good."

"Okay, Miss Ranch Boss! We'll have Bucky fixed in no time." Chad retrieved the hose, a scrub brush, and Skye's bucket.

Standing several feet back from Champ, Skye kept an eye on Chad while she stared at the sorrel's sparkling coat. The horse's blaze and four socks looked like they had just been painted a glistening white. His long, silky mane and tail blew gently in the soft summer breeze.

"You are one beautiful hunk!" Skye said.

"Thanks!" Chad turned back and winked.

In vain, Skye looked for the closest groundhog hole in which to crawl. The summer sun, beating mercilessly, was a far second place to the heat radiating from her face once again. In one quick action, she grabbed a lead rope from a hook on the barn, snapped it onto her horse's halter, and turned Champ in the direction of the paddock gate. "C'mon, boy! How about some lunch in the pasture?"

*Squirt!* A shot of ice-cold hose water struck Skye's back.

"Hey!" Skye jerked Champ to a stop and spun toward Chad.

Conveniently busy with Bucky's hoof, Chad glanced up, the familiar devilish grin lighting up his face. "What's the matter? Cat got your tongue?" he joked.

"Very funny." Skye led Champ to the gate, swung it open, and released her horse into the pasture. She tiptoed back to Chad and stood over his bent frame.

*Splash!* Skye emptied the bucket of soapy water all over Chad's back and took off.

"Yikes!" he yelled.

A safe distance away, Skye stopped, pointed at Chad, and doubled over in laughter. There he stood, drenched and dripping, his Stetson the only dry spot on him.

"What's the matter?" Skye teased. "Cat got your tongue?"

"Why, you little brat!" Chad grabbed the hose, chasing Skye and soaking her relentlessly with long jets of icy water.

"Please! Don't!" Skye yelled. "I'm getting—"

"Cloud, my Cloud in the Sky! I'll help you, my sweetest girlfriend!" a voice shrieked from the back door of the house.

Down through the yard barreled a roly-poly sixteen-year-old boy dressed in a full cowboy suit with ten-gallon hat, boots, and two toy pistols in holsters. "I'll save you, my lovely queen!" he yelled at the top of his lungs.

"Oh, no!" Skye yelled. Stopping dead in her tracks, she stood while Chad's hose continued to soak her from head to toe. "Joey, not now!"

## chapter two

Skye and Chad stood, mouths wide open. Joey charged into the paddock, ripped the hose out of Chad's hand, threw it on the ground, and ran to Skye. "I'll save you from that beast!" he proclaimed, wrapping his arms around her in a full bear hug.

"Stop it!" Skye yelled. "I'm okay! Let me go!"

Paying no heed, Joey picked Skye up like a sack of potatoes, carried her out of the paddock, and dumped her on the backyard lawn. There Skye sat, a lump of dripping hair, soaking wet clothes, and fuming temper.

"Joey!" she screamed when she barely had recovered her breath.

With surprising balance, Joey spun on a dime. He drew his two six-shooters and made a beeline back to Chad, who beamed with a this-is-too-funny smirk in Skye's direction.

"I'm the sheriff in these here parts," Joey declared as he stood an arm's length from Chad, "and don'tcha dare move. I gotcha covered."

Chad, barely able to contain himself, raised his hands in mock full surrender. "Don't shoot, Sheriff. I give up."

Out of the barn came Morgan carrying a bottle of hydrogen peroxide on her lap. "What's happening?" she asked, heading straight for Skye. "And what are you doing on the ground?"

From the back door of the house a familiar voice yelled, "Joey, we're not done with your lesson!" Down through the yard, Mr. Chambers tore toward the sheriff. "Skye," Mr. Chambers huffed as he raced by, "I'm sorry about this. Joey went AWOL on bathroom break. Are you hurt?"

"Not exactly," Skye grumbled as she stood. Folding her arms tightly, she gave Joey a look that could have soured milk. "But he shows up at the worst times!"

Morgan started giggling.

"What's so funny?" Skye blurted out as Morgan and the others quickly got the brunt of Skye's sour look.

Mr. Chambers patted Joey on the back. "Nice job, Sheriff. I see you caught another one. But we need to go back in the house now, okay?"

"Should we stick 'im in jail, Mr. C.?" Joey holstered his pistols and squared his humongous hat on his bent ears. His beet red cheeks beamed with pride. "I can guard him all day long."

"Oh, please don't." Chad went along with the charade. "I'll be real good."

"Oh, please!" Skye fumed. "This is so lame. I'm outta here!" She swept her straggled hair back off her face and stomped into the house.

Monday morning and the first day of riding lessons for the students arrived too soon. Already the entire summer had been ruined, as far as Skye was concerned, and it had just begun.

"I've never been so humiliated in my whole life!" she had complained to Morgan the night before. Now,

16

to make matters worse, Mr. and Mrs. Chambers had assigned Joey to Skye for all of his lessons. Aunt Dot in Charleston was looking better by the second!

Inside the barn on this gorgeous June day, Mr. Chambers, Morgan, and Chad were already busy showing three students how to groom their horses.

Skye and Mrs. Chambers were in the paddock tacking Champ and Bucky in their western gear.

Joey, in his cowboy outfit and rider's helmet, stood on the opposite side of the paddock, examining the hinges on the gate. Engrossed in their purpose and function, he swung the gate open and closed, open and closed, open and closed ...

"Mom," Skye said under her breath as she adjusted Champ's bridle, "why are you making me do this?"

"Do what, honey?" Mrs. Chambers maintained a neutral expression while throwing a saddle across Bucky's back.

"You know I can't stand Joey. We just don't hit it off. So why did you and Dad pair me up with *him*?"

Mrs. Chambers pulled Bucky's cinch strap tight and secured it. "You two don't hit it off? Hmm, I never got that impression. I thought Joey simply adored you."

"That's the problem!" Skye faced Mrs. Chambers. "He follows me around like a puppy, and tells me that he loves me, and calls me 'Cloud, his girlfriend,' and everybody thinks that's so cute, but I—I could just die. He makes me feel like ... well, I just don't want to work with him. That's all."

Mrs. Chambers stepped back from Bucky and looked at Skye. Even in her Stetson's shade, the woman's deep blue eyes sparkled. "Honey, we believe it will be good for you to work with Joey for several reasons. Number one: Joey listens to you really well. Number two: Champ and Bucky are so similar in their training, it will be easy for the two horses to work together. Number three: since

17

Joey's here at Keystone Stables for a second time, he's what we call 'advanced.' And, Skye, you *are* our advanced student teacher."

"And?" Somehow, Skye felt there was more to their decision. She turned toward Champ and started adjusting his cinch.

Mrs. Chambers touched Skye on the shoulder, and Skye slowly turned toward the woman. "I'm sure you recall Pastor Newman's latest series of sermons on First Corinthians chapter thirteen. A Christian who doesn't allow God to love through him—or her—is a poor example of what a Christian should be. Here you have an opportunity to really share Christ's love. Because of Joey's Down syndrome, he may never completely understand all about God and salvation and what it means, but he can feel Christ's love through others. Through you."

Deep in thought, Skye stared at the ground and adjusted her helmet's strap.

Mrs. Chambers raised Skye's chin, and Skye met the woman's blue eyes again.

"Will you at least give it a try, for us ... and for the Lord? That's all we ask."

"Oh, all right," Skye conceded. "I'll try."

"Good girl." Mrs. Chambers' face lit up. "It might not be that bad. Remember, Champ will be right here with you the whole time."

"Cloud, my girlfriend!" Joey yelled as he came running up to Skye. "Is it time to ride the horsey now? I'm all dressed. See?" Pride written all over his face, the boy glanced down at his clothes. He stroked his brand-new checkered shirt, finally grasping a gigantic tin star pinned to his chest. "I'm an official sheriff too. That's what this here badge says. An official sheriff has to know how to ride a horsey. So let's get goin', okay? Cloud, my girlfriend, I love you. And Jesus loves you too!"

"See?" Skye directed her question to Mrs. Chambers.

Mrs. Chambers tightened Bucky's cinch one more time then smiled at Joey. "Young man, I know you're excited about getting started. We've got big plans for you this summer."

"Like what, Mrs. C.?" Joey's eyes lit up with the thought of any kind of surprise.

Skye abruptly turned her back to Joey as she checked Champ's gear once more, tightening the cinch and adjusting the bridle's cheek strap.

"Well," Mrs. Chambers said, "since you went through all the beginner's lessons last year, you're going to learn a whole lot of brand-new things, such as how to canter on a lunging line, how to square up a horse, how to shave a horse's whiskers—"

"Ooh," Joey's voice bubbled with excitement and he clapped his hands. "I saw Mr. C. do that last year. That makes the horsies look so-o-o pretty. You mean, I get to do that?"

"Yep," Mrs. Chambers answered. "But the first thing you're going to do today is take your first trail ride with Skye." She untied Bucky from the fence and handed the reins to Joey. "Here's your horse. You remember Bucky from last year, don't you?"

Joey pushed the reins back into Mrs. Chambers' hands, shuffled to Champ's side, and grabbed the saddle's horn. "But I don't wanna ride Bucky. I wanna ride Cloud's horsey. I wanna ride Champ!"

Like a lightning bolt, Skye pushed herself between Champ and Joey, forcing the boy back. She glared pitchforks at him and made a declaration that left no question of her intent. "Nobody but me rides my horse!"

## chapter three

S kye ..." Mrs. Chambers whispered a soft reprimand. Folding her arms, Skye stood like a fortress. A brick wall couldn't have said it better. "I'm going *nowhere* without Champ!"

Joey's eyes watered, and he was ready to cry. "Don'tcha want me to — to ride your horsey, Cloud?" he stammered. "I—I won't hurt him."

"Young lady, we'll discuss this later," Mrs. Chambers said in no uncertain terms. She touched Joey's shoulder and directed him gently toward the buckskin. "Aw, Joey, I think Bucky's feelings would really be hurt if you didn't ride him."

The horse glanced back and nickered.

"See?" Mrs. Chambers said. "I think he remembers you. He wants to take *you* on a nice ride through the woods. What do you say?"

"Okay!" Joey's face brightened as he wiped his watery eyes. "He sure is a pretty horsey, ain't he?"

"He sure is. Now let me help you mount," Mrs. Chambers said. "Grab the horn while I hold Bucky steady for you."

"Okay, Mrs. C.!" Joey beamed and then climbed onto the horse.

Skye wasted no time grabbing Champ's reins and mounting.

Mrs. Chambers turned toward Skye and gently stroked Champ's neck. "Joey probably would love to see Piney Hollow again. That will take less than an hour to ride out there and back. Now, what do you say, Skye?"

As usual, when a tough challenge wound her into a tight knot, Skye chewed her lower lip. Her glance shifted from Mrs. Chambers to the bottom of the field, zeroing in on the trail through the woods that led to the campsite. *Even with Joey that'll be cool,* she reasoned. Without a word, she stared at Mrs. Chambers.

"Skye?" Mrs. Chambers said.

"Okay." Skye let out a stingy smile as she reined Champ. "No problem. Let's go, Joey."

"Have a great time!" Mrs. Chambers said, swinging open the paddock gate.

Back to lip chewing, Skye took the lead down through the field and focused on the task that lay before her. As Joey rambled on and on about his lovely queen, Skye stroked Champ's neck and did her best to fulfill the promise she'd made to Mrs. Chambers. "Champ," she said under her breath, "I don't know what I'd do without you." Then she smiled all the way into the woods.

Weeks passed, and Skye was at war with herself. It had been months since she'd felt so confused about anything.

Since she had accepted Christ, Skye and her feelings had been getting along quite well, she reasoned. But where was God in her life lately? He had always been there for her, and with her. But now, with the way she felt about Joey, God seemed so far away. She absolutely hated the way she felt, but she just couldn't help it.

Without success, Skye tried to remember the last time she had made a point to pray—about Joey or anything. And how about reading the Bible? Right now, she wasn't even sure where her Bible was. Her bedroom had become a hideaway of frustration where she punched pillows and cried. Outside her room, she endured Joey, who never let her out of his sight. Horseback riding? Picnics? Board games during family time in the evenings? Joey was right there next to Skye. Every free minute she could find, Skye stowed away in the barn with Champ, the only one who seemed to really understand.

With an attitude as sour as a rotten grapefruit, Skye found herself in frequent mother-daughter discussions with Mrs. C. But even the threat of groundings didn't help Skye snap out of her sullen mood. On the calendar in her bedroom, she scored a huge red X on the day in August when Joey would leave Keystone Stables. Skye lived for that day.

Skye also lived for Sunday school and her teen class more than ever. She cherished the time when Joey attended his own class. However, her joy was short-lived.

In the church service, as usual, the Keystone Stables family and students filled an entire row. Without fail, Joey managed to squeeze himself in next to Skye. Total embarrassment arrived like clockwork when Joey would blurt out during chorus time every single Sunday, "My birthday's in September!" While the pastor humored Joey, Skye would slide down in the pew, turn red-hot, and bury her face in her hands. The humiliation was almost too much to bear.

Now Tuesday morning had arrived, and Skye was thrilled for a very special reason. No working with Joey today!

The farmers' market at the Snyder County Auction Grounds beckoned, and although all the new students were going, Skye hoped for the best. "Maybe today will be the start of my new life," she joked with Morgan as the two sat in the backseat of the traveling minivan. "Maybe Joey'll get lost."

As the van pulled into the market, the students exploded with chatter about the prospects of an exciting time. Joey, buckled in the seat in front of Skye, glanced back, wiggled his fingers and smiled, and squared his cowboy hat firmly just as Mr. Chambers always did. "Where are we, Mr. C.?" Joey yelled as he turned and looked out the side window.

"At a place full of food and fun," Mr. Chambers answered. "Keister's Flea and Farmers' Market!"

"Ooh," Joey yelled, "I don't like fleas. They itch!"

"They don't itch," another student said, "but they bite! My dog told me that once."

Mrs. Chambers looked back and smiled. "Kids, there are no fleas for sale. But wait until you see all the veggies, toys, and other things on display. You'll love this place."

Skye folded her arms and glanced out the window, her heart racing with the thought of horse models of all shapes and sizes.

Morgan's words were packed with excitement. "Skye, what are you hunting for today? I'm going to see if there are any bargains on computer games. Remember last month when I found that old Star Wars game for just a dollar? Now, that's a deal—and one that fits my budget."

As the van joined a caravan of vehicles creeping at a snail's pace to park, Skye's eyes darted wildly.

On both sides of the road, vendors were selling their wares. Mounds of fresh cauliflower, broccoli, carrots, cabbage, and baskets of fresh fruit covered tabletops. Dozens of other tables, under canopies, displayed baseball cards, stuffed animals, old sleds, dolls, antique lamps, and used clothing. Adjoined to the backs of the stands were rows of trucks, vans, and Amish buggies, resting from their earlier arrival and hasty unloading.

Eager vendors were making their pitch to a steady flow of shoppers. Other marketers lounged in the shade of their beach umbrellas. Hands folded on rounded bellies, they scrutinized every person who came near their wares.

The shoppers, some already toting heavy bags, milled around the tables like ants after sugar cubes. Sunburned farmers in baseball caps mingled with plump ladies in tank tops and shorts. Wide-eyed children stared and, when mothers turned their backs, touched every toy they could reach.

As usual, the market had drawn Amish folk from nearby farms. Bearded men in straw hats, white shirts, and black pants exchanged the latest news in Pennsylvania Dutch dialect. Their women—dressed in white caps, granny glasses, royal blue dresses, black aprons, and work boots—chatted in circles. Their children, carbon copies of the parents, stood close to the adults and eyed the tables with wonder. Keister's market was definitely the place to be!

Mr. Chambers drove the van onto a large field and found a place in one of the long rows of parked vehicles. Skye glanced back at the marketplace and spotted a table crowded with horse models of all shapes and sizes. She popped up in her seat as if she'd sat on a tack.

"Horses!" she said as she pressed her nose flat against the window. "Morgan, look. There's a table loaded with horses. That's where I'm heading."

"Good," Morgan replied. "I'm heading in the same direction."

In less than five minutes, Mr. Chambers had the van unloaded and had everyone ready to go, including Morgan in her Jazzy.

Skye did a quick mental review of her horse collection. Again, her heart raced with the prospect of finding another horse, one completely different from all the others. "Mom," she said, slipping her fingers through her hair, "can Morgan and I go by ourselves?"

Joey rushed to Skye's side and grabbed her hand. "Cloud, my girlfriend, kin I go with you? Nobody'll hurtcha today. See, I'm the sheriff." Under his ten-gallon hat, full red cheeks blew on the star on his chest. Joey then radiated an effortless smile.

"I don't think so," Skye said, quickly pulling her hand free. "Why don't you—"

"Joey," Mr. Chambers said as he reached his arm around the boy's shoulders, "Mrs. C. and I want to show you and the other guys something really neat inside the barn. Do you like rabbits?"

"Wabbits? Ooh, yeah. They're really fuzzy and cute. I love wabbits."

Mr. Chambers turned Joey toward the other students. "Well, then let's go. We have a lot to see today."

Walking away with the group, Mrs. Chambers looked back at Skye and Morgan. "Girls, be back here at one o'clock."

"Okay, Mom!" Skye yelled.

"One o'clock!" Morgan added as the two headed in the opposite direction.

Melding into the crowd, the girls flowed with the river of passersby. Skye's eyes darted wildly as she tried to look in every direction at once. The humid air, filled with the chatter of making a good deal, already clung to the girls like a sticky cloth. The hint of grilling hot dogs and french fries also hung in the haze, with faint wafts of horse manure infiltrating the food smells throughout the entire grounds.

A half hour and a soda later brought the girls to a table piled high with old records in their jackets, VHS tapes, and used computer games.

"This is the table I saw on the way in." Morgan's freckles danced with a radiant smile. "Look at all these games."

But Skye had something else on her mind. Glancing across the road, she spotted her target on the right. "Hey, over there are the horses, about six tables on the other side."

"You go ahead ..." Morgan never looked up from a game box she was studying. "I'll catch up with you in a while."

Skye glanced at her watch, smiled, and took off toward the table. *Two more hours!*

At the horse table, children as well as adults had lined up like cows at a water trough. Skye excused herself and squeezed right up front. The vendor, sitting in a lawn chair in the shade of his truck, let out a lazy yawn and scratched his curly white hair. *Hmm,* Skye thought, *he must know horses are in. I guess he doesn't need to "sell."*

Skye studied the display, her heart pounding like a hammer in her chest. On her left, she saw a shoebox filled with dozens of tiny plastic horses in an array of equine colors. Next to the box stood a row of the tiniest crystal glass horses, probably not new, but very nice. In the center stood three Breyer stallions, one white, one brown, one black. On the right stood a cluster of inch-high polished-stone ponies, and next to those stood six large plastic dappled grays with saddles and chain bridles. Each in its own box, they stood almost a foot tall and were brand-new.

"Wow!" Skye said to herself. "I don't have any dappled grays, and no horse as big as these either!" Picking up a box, she searched for a price. She glanced at the owner who had not moved but now watched Skye like a hawk.

Pointing at the box, she smiled.

*Four!* The vendor raised his fingers but barely lifted his hand off his stomach.

Skye did some quick figuring as she reached into her pocket. *Five dollars minus a soda equals four fifty,* she reasoned. *I can live on fifty cents for the rest of the week. I gotta have that horse.*

Before her next thought, Skye found the vendor standing right in front of her and eyeing her money like it was gold.

One plastic horse richer, Skye clutched the box as if *it* were made of gold and turned just as Morgan came motoring toward her.

"Hey, Skye," she said, "you should see the neat game I got—hey! Look behind you. There's Mrs. C. She looks worried, and she's in an awful hurry. She's coming this way."

"Mom, what's the matter?" Skye asked as the three stepped away from the table and out of the flow of traffic.

"Have you seen Joey?" Mrs. Chambers' face pleaded for a positive response.

"No," Morgan said. "We thought he was with you guys."

"He was," Mrs. Chambers said. "But we let the boys go to the bathroom inside the barn. We waited and waited for Joey, but he didn't come out. Finally, Tom went in and discovered a back door that he never knew was there. Joey must have gotten disoriented and slipped out that way. He's missing. I'm on my way to report this to the main office. In the meantime, you two go up and down every row of tables in this section, and check between the cars in the parking lot. We've *got* to find him."

"Sure, Mrs. C.," Morgan said, pivoting toward the crowd. "Come on, Skye. Let's go."

Mrs. Chambers turned. "If you find him, bring him to the office. I'm sure they have a loudspeaker system here. You can let us know that way. Report there in fifteen minutes whether you find him or not."

Skye shoved the horse under her arm, and her insides erupted with selfish anger. "Well, this is just great," she said, her face shriveling up like a moldy prune. "Joey's not even with me today, and he's still managing to ruin my life!"

*chapter four*

"Will you get a life!" Rare as a snowstorm in July, sweet, calm Morgan gave Skye a piece of her mind. "Joey could be hurt, or he could be wandering out near the highway. We have to find him."

"Hey, I didn't think of that," Skye admitted. "As usual, you're right. Let's split up. We can cover more ground that way. I'll do this whole lower end with all the vendors and food stands. Do you want to check the parking lot?"

Morgan had already turned her wheelchair in that direction. "Sure thing. I'll get that done in a jiff. I'll meet you at the office in fifteen minutes."

"Okay. Maybe Mom and Dad will have found him by then, and they'll be there waiting. He's probably standing in a corner of the barn, staring holes through some animals."

"I sure hope so." Morgan started edging her way into the flow.

Skye shoved her fingers through her hair, let out a frustrated sigh, and set out to find Joey. Weaving in and out of the crowd, she checked every stand on both sides of the road. But the market's wares were fascinating, and her eyes wandered again, focusing every now and then on the menagerie of items up for sale.

Skye glanced at her watch. Ten minutes had passed and no sign of Joey. As she headed toward the food stands, Skye's conscience pricked her. *We've got to find that kid,* she told herself.

Then she spotted something.

At the last vendor on Skye's left, a magnificent display of halters, bridles, and blankets in a rainbow of colors caught her eye. In the center of three tables, an Amish man stood, polishing a brand-new stainless-steel bit. Next to the buggy in the back a plump woman sat, garbed in black, stitching a red and white blanket. With dress, bib, and cap strings smothering her neck, the woman's full cheeks matched the red on the blanket as sweat beads trickled down her face. After every few stitches, she poked at her glasses, which insisted on creeping to the end of her nose and thwarting her delicate work.

"Wow!" Skye stared at the blanket in the woman's hands. "Would Champ ever look good in that!"

Making her way to the table, Skye feasted her eyes on the display. Picturing Champ tacked in all the fancy gear, Skye completely forgot why she was there. She picked up a black leather halter and inspected its fine tan stitching and shiny brass parts. Abruptly, someone grabbed her from behind.

"Cloud, my girlfriend!" Joey shouted in Skye's ear. "I found you. You were lost, weren'tcha?"

"Oh, Joey! You're here!" Skye said as her nerves jumped. Pulling away from the boy, she quickly dropped the halter. As she did, Joey spun her around and sucked her into his chest.

"I—I love you, Cloud," Joey babbled and kissed her cheek like he was sucking lemons. "You should be more careful so that you don't get lost!"

29

Boisterous Joey attracted an audience like a barker at a state fair. Passersby stared, children giggled, and Skye turned red-hot. Pulling away again, she glared at his smiling cheeks smeared with ketchup.

"Cut it out, Joey!" Skye pleaded, wiping slobbery ketchup off her face. "Where have you been? Everybody's looking for you. Come on. We need to go to the — "

"Well, if it isn't Skye Nicholson!" a cocky voice sang from behind, and the words stuck in Skye's back like poison darts. "I haven't seen you since you were pleasantly removed from Madison!"

Skye turned. There in all her brazen glory, in the best summer clothes money could buy, stood the one and only Miss Snoot of Madison Middle. With her were two other girls, noses stuck high in the air.

*Hannah Gilbert!* Skye's face burned with fire, her eyes darting in all directions. *If I* ever *needed a rock to crawl under, it's right now!*

"Who's your boyfriend, Skye?" Hannah flipped back her long blonde curls and lifted her nose to match her two friends'. "Someone you met at camp?" The other girls hissed like vipers stalking their prey.

"For *your* information," Skye said, flipping back her own hair, Hannah-style, "he's just one of our summer students. I'm babysitting, if you have to know."

"Cloud's my girlfriend!" Joey chimed in. "Are you Cloud's friends? Cloud says she has lots of friends."

"Y-e-s-s-s," Hannah said with a sarcastic flair, "we're all *Cloud's* friends, aren't we, girls?"

"Best friends, in fact," one of the other girls spewed out.

"I like all Cloud's friends!" Joey bubbled. Before Hannah knew what was coming, Joey wrapped his arms around her and planted a slobbery, ketchupy kiss on her cheek. "That's not really true," he announced. "I *love* Cloud's friends, and Jesus loves you too."

Hannah's friends stood, eyes like saucers, mouths hanging open.

Skye folded her arms and a go-Joey-go smile spread all over her face. *Serves her right! She needs a good dose of her own snooty medicine.* "Give the other girls a kiss too!" Skye said.

"Yuck!" Hannah screamed, pulling herself out of Joey's clutches. "Let me go, you big ape!"

Hannah's friends backed away, their faces layered with a strange facade of makeup and panic. "Ah, we've got to go ... right, Hannah?" Each one grabbed Hannah and started pulling her away.

"You'll pay for this, Skye Nicholson!" Hannah said, yanking one arm free and wiping her face. "You better watch your back!"

Skye raised her hand and wiggled her fingers in a mock farewell. "See you at the horse show!" she yelled.

Up the three girls' noses went. They huffed themselves away as Hannah viciously wiped her face.

Joey lifted his cowboy hat and scratched his head. "Cloud, why'd she call me 'a big ape'? There ain't no monkeys in my family."

"Aw, forget it." For the first time in her life, Skye was glad that Joey was with her. "She's just ignorant, that's all. Let's go."

"Where're we goin'?" Joey asked.

"Over to the main office. We have to find Mom and Dad and the other kids. They're all lost too. Come on."

"Okay!" Joey said. "This is fun. But kin I get a drink first? I'm really thirsty."

Skye spotted a soda stand off to the side. "Sure. We'll get a drink then find everybody else. Come on."

Sipping his straw in a quart-sized cup, Joey trailed after Skye as she headed toward the main office. From a distance, Skye spotted Mr. and Mrs. Chambers and the other students waiting outside the door.

"I've got him!" Skye yelled and waved. "Mom, I found him!"

Mrs. Chambers waved, and in seconds the group joined Skye and Joey.

"Hi, everybody!" Joey said after a large sip of soda.

"Thank the Lord," Mrs. Chambers said. "And Skye, thanks. You did a good job. I knew I could count on you. Where's Morgan?"

"Here I am!" Morgan yelled, joining the group from behind.

Mrs. Chambers studied Joey's face. "From the looks of you, young man, it's not too hard to figure out where you were."

"Yeah, he was down in the food section all right," Skye said. "But let's make one minor change in my story. I didn't find him. He found me."

## chapter five

O
h, give me a home,
    Where the buffalo roam,
        And I'll show you a carpet that stinks!"

At a Saturday morning cookout, Chad strummed his guitar while he sang his own version of "Home on the Range." Around the Piney Hollow campfire with Chad sat Joey and the other summer students, laughing hysterically and holding their sides. Skye giggled at Chad too while she cracked eggs into a large black skillet on the open fire. Mr. Chambers, in a chef's hat and red apron, was bent over the pan, scrambling the eggs. Tippy and Tyler, the two West Highland terriers, sat with the students and eyed the cooking eggs. Mrs. Chambers and Morgan were busy at a nearby table, pouring orange juice and setting places for the hungry students.

Under a clump of scrub pines near the chuck wagon, Champ and the five other Keystone Stables horses rested from their crack-of-dawn trail ride. Next to the horses, the parked ranch truck toted a beverage cooler and boxes of breakfast supplies.

The sky, although still a curtain of pink, was fast giving way to a brilliant, cloudless blue, the promise of another hot summer day.

"Okay, kids!" Mr. Chambers said as he used both hands to lift the heavy pan and carry it to the center of the table. "The eggs are ready. Time to chow down!"

"Yes, come and get it!" Mrs. Chambers finished pouring juice into a paper cup. "Morgan, make sure everyone gets a wet wipe."

"Sure thing, Mrs. C." Morgan grabbed a container off the table and handed out wet cloths as everyone gathered around the table.

Skye eyed Chad's every move and hurried to the table to sit next to him. As she sat, Joey charged the table and flopped into the chair on her other side. As usual, his bright red cheeks beamed pure excitement from under his ten-gallon hat.

"Kin I sit next to Cloud, my girlfriend?" Joey asked. He reached his arm around Skye and gave her a kiss on the cheek. "I love her, ya know."

"Ooh, Joey loves her," a camper mocked.

Other students snickered while they sat in their places. "And he's kissing her too!" one exclaimed.

Mrs. Chambers poured coffee for her husband. "Ah, Joey, maybe you should sit—"

"It's okay, Mom," Skye said.

Mr. and Mrs. Chambers, Morgan, and Chad all exchanged startled looks.

"I owe this kid a big one," Skye started to explain. "He helped me out of a jam with Hannah Gilbert at the market on Tuesday."

"Skye, hold on a minute," Mr. Chambers interrupted. "Let's pray, and while we're eating, you can fill us in."

Skye bowed her head, glanced at Joey, and smiled.

" ... and, Lord, thank you for this beautiful place and all this wonderful food. In Jesus' name. Amen."

Mr. Chambers finished his prayer and smoothed down his mustache. "Now let's dig into the best breakfast this side of heaven." He stood and started spooning large portions of scrambled eggs onto all the plates. Mrs. Chambers served a basket of fresh-baked biscuits while Morgan passed a plate piled high with crispy, brown bacon.

Joey's eyes glistened as he stared at his full plate. "Ooh, I just love eggs and bacon."

"And scrambled eggs are the best," a student said as he stuffed a spoonful into his mouth. "I tried a raw egg once, but I didn't like it."

"Raw eggs? Yuck!" another student said.

Mrs. Chambers set the biscuit basket down and sipped her coffee. "Now, Skye, what did you want to tell us about Joey and Hannah?"

While everyone dug into the food, Skye began. "I meant to tell you, but I forgot. Morgan knows about it, though. At the market on Tuesday, Joey and I ran into Hannah and two of her friends. You know how snooty she is —"

"Skye ..." Mrs. Chambers said.

"Sorry, but she is," Skye said. "Anyway, she said something really ignorant about me and Joey, and then guess what happened?"

"If I know Joey, I think I know what's coming." Mr. Chambers chuckled and then took a bite of biscuit.

Chad's dimpled smile lit up his whole face. "Joey can be *real* friendly, even to strangers."

Skye started giggling. "You guessed it. He grabbed Hannah and gave her the biggest, sloppiest kiss she's probably ever gotten from anyone. She and her friends were horrified. You showed her, didn't you, Joey?"

"Yeah, I showed her that I love her. I love all of Cloud's friends. I wanted to show the other girls too, but they were in a hurry to go."

Morgan's eyes danced as she smiled. "I would've given a month's allowance to see Hannah's face. Definitely a historical moment—maybe even hysterical."

"Now, girls," Mrs. Chambers said, "just remember to be kind to people like Hannah. Inside all of that show and glitter might be a troubled young lady. Fancy clothes and a big house don't bring happiness."

"That's right," Mr. Chambers added. "She might be a very lonely girl. Maybe sometime you'll have the opportunity to share the love of Christ with her. Just be ready when that time comes."

"I don't think she's interested in God at all," Skye said. "I've never heard her talk about church or anything like that."

Mr. Chambers sipped his coffee. "All the more reason you need to be ready. Skye, don't look at her as the enemy. Look at her as someone who might need help."

"I helped her!" Joey threw in. "I hugged her and told her I loved her. That should've made her feel good!"

"I don't know if that made her feel good," Skye said with a smirk, "but I have an idea that she felt different— very different."

The annual Snyder County Horse Show in August was the highlight of the summer, and this year Joey would be competing! Pleased with the boy's progress, Mr. and Mrs. Chambers had decided to enter him in a new Special-Needs Beginners' Western Pleasure class. In this class, each rider had to lead his horse and square him up, ride him at a walk and then trot around the corral, turn him, and back him. Joey looked forward to every practice he had with Skye, and Saturday was no exception.

After the Piney Hollow cookout, Skye, Champ, Joey, and Bucky stood in the practice field, getting ready to work on Joey's routine.

After she cleaned the horses' hooves and helped Joey mount, Skye climbed onto Champ. Chad was in the paddock teaching another student how to tack a horse when he and Skye caught each other's eye.

"Hey, Skye," Chad yelled, "how's Bucky's thrush? I see you're still pouring peroxide on that bad foot."

"We just have to keep after it," Skye yelled back. "It flared up, but I think as long as we keep the peroxide on it, he'll be okay."

"Good," Chad said. "Oh, I wanted to tell you that I have the evening free. I'd like to stay and shoot some pool. Do you think Mr. and Mrs. C. would mind?"

*Well, I sure wouldn't!* Skye's face glowed with delight. "Of course they wouldn't mind. You're always welcome here."

"Great," he said. "I'll see you later then."

"Later," Skye said, turning Champ toward the open field. With her heart racing and her brain exploding with thoughts of Chad, she forced herself to refocus. "Joey, just like we've done so many times before, we're going to practice what you'll be doing in the horse show. I want you and Bucky to follow Champ and me."

"Okay, Cloud." Joey turned Bucky and lined up behind Skye and her horse. "But I wanna ride Champ today. Could I please ride Champ? I've always wanted to ride Champ."

Skye took a deep breath, ready to give Joey a blast. Then she remembered Hannah. "Well," she said politely, "maybe sometime you can ride Champ, but not today. You have too much to teach Bucky. He needs you. Okay?"

"Okay, Cloud," Joey conceded.

For the next hour, Skye and Champ rehearsed with Joey and his horse. Around the practice field they went, starting, stopping, dismounting, and mounting. Although Joey listened well, the practice was far from what Skye had planned. For the umpteenth time after he got off

37

Bucky, Joey asked the same old question, "Kin I ride Champ now?"

Patience was never one of Skye Nicholson's virtues, and after an hour of Joey's nagging, the whole humorous Hannah incident had disappeared into thin air. By the time the session ended, Skye was fuming big time.

At the paddock fence, Skye stopped Champ abruptly, jumped off the horse without even bothering to use her stirrup, and ripped off her helmet. "Joey, park Bucky right here next to Champ and dismount. Your lesson for today is *over!*" Lost in her own selfish thoughts, she barely noticed Chad still working with another student in the small corral.

"Okay, Cloud." Joey got off Bucky and tied him to the fence. "Now kin I ride Champ?"

*Boom!* Skye's temper erupted like a volcano. In a flash, she whirled around at Joey and shoved her index finger right into his face, ready to give him a piece of her mind.

*"He can't help it."* Mrs. Chambers' words from a counseling session flashed in Skye's mind, and she stopped dead in her tracks.

"Ooh, you look mad, Cloud," Joey said, backing away. "I didn't mean to make you mad. I'm sorry."

Skye took a deep breath and gave Joey her best smile. "Nah, Joey, that's okay," she said sincerely. "But you can't ride Champ today. He's tired. Okay?"

"Okay, Cloud," Joey said, beaming his best smile back. "But kin I ride him now?"

ll right!" Morgan cheered. "I sank one of her subs!" While Joey and the other students played table games with Mr. and Mrs. Chambers in the dining room, Skye, Morgan, and Chad played computer games in the basement. The walls vibrated with the noise of electronic laser blasts and explosions. Tippy and Ty lay on the floor, totally engrossed in chewing their own play toys.

*You lost! You lost!* A sinister voice declared as Chad's screen flashed the words in brilliant colors. *Wanna try again or are you CHICKEN?*

"Give me a break," Chad said to the screen and then turned to Skye. "Hey, how about a game of pool? This *Chicken* game isn't working for me."

Skye, happy that Joey was nowhere near, giggled while she worked her controls. "Sure. I'm bombing out on my game too. Maybe I'll have better luck with pool balls."

"Then let's do it," Chad said.

"Morgan, do you mind?" Skye shut down her computer.

"No problem," Morgan said. "I've just connected with a kid from Australia in this *Battleship* game. She's a

Christian too. We're discussing life while we're trying to wipe out each other's fleet. This is too cool."

Chad headed toward the pool table. "I'll rack the balls, Skye. You can break them."

*He is so-o-o polite.* Skye grabbed a pool stick from the wall mount. "Okay, but I'm not very good at this. I've had only a few lessons."

Chad grabbed a stick and chalked its tip. "As a beginner, all you need to remember is to hit the cue ball in the center. You don't want to stab at it or hit it too low. That'll make it skip across the table at the same time your stick is gouging the cloth on the table. That's disaster."

"Dad tells me that all the time," Skye said, chalking her cue tip. With a nervous eye on Chad, she placed the cue ball on the table and took aim, holding the stick as Mr. Chambers had taught her.

"Easy, now," Chad whispered. "Take your time and hit the ball in the center."

Skye pulled back, and *whack!* She miscued, and the ball went flying into a corner pocket. The triangular rack of balls sat on the table undisturbed.

"Oh, no!" Skye squealed. "I think I missed."

"No problem." Chad retrieved the cue ball and rolled it back to Skye. "Try it again. We're not in a world championship or anything."

*He is so-o-o kind.* Skye smiled in agreement. "Okay. One more time." She took aim and hit the ball squarely. It smacked the racked set, scattering balls all over the table. A cherry red ball dropped into a side pocket.

"The three ball! You did it!" Chad said. "Very good, Skye. Are you sure you haven't been on a world billiards tour?"

Skye giggled at Chad. "Wow, that's the best shot I ever made."

"Well, you have another turn." Chad pointed to a yellow-and-white ball near a corner pocket. "And look here. The nine is just hanging on the end. That's an easy shot. Go for it."

"Okay, Mr. Billiard Boss!" Skye smiled at Chad and ran her fingers through her hair, winding long strands around her ear. Carefully, she took aim and made the shot.

"You're on a roll now." Chad smiled. "You have a run of two. That's pretty good for a beginner."

"What should I do now?" Skye couldn't help but stare at Chad's wavy blond hair.

He walked around the table, studying the layout of the balls. "I think—"

*Bam! Bam!* A knock at the basement door drew all eyes in that direction. As though launched by giant slingshots, the dogs charged the door with a barrage of guard-dog warnings.

"Will somebody get the door, please?" Mr. Chambers yelled from outside.

"Here, boys!" Skye yelled.

"Come here, boys. It's just Mr. C.," Morgan added.

Chad hurried toward the door. "Coming!"

Tippy and Ty retreated, releasing long ripples of suspicious growls.

Mr. Chambers shuffled in, lugging an enormous computer monitor. "Chad, will you open my office door? This old thing weighs a ton."

"Sure thing, Mr. C." Chad reached toward a second door off to the side.

The dogs waddled to Mr. Chambers and greeted him with wagging tails.

"Thanks, Chad," Mr. Chambers said. "George just dropped off this antique. Looks like I'll have my work cut out trying to fix it." He huffed his way into the computer shop. "I don't think I can get the parts for it anymore. Maybe I can talk him into getting a flat panel. It might cost him as much to get this fixed as to buy a new one."

41

"That does look ancient," Chad said, walking back to the pool table. "Now, where were we, Skye?"

Skye stared into Chad's brown eyes and her heart melted. *He is so-o-o cool.* "You were going to tell me which ball to shoot next."

"Oh, I almost forgot!" Mr. Chambers stuck his head out through the office doorway. "Eileen said the pizza'll be ready in about fifteen minutes."

"Pizza! Yes!" Morgan yelled. "The perfect end to a perfect day."

Chad pointed to a blue ball. "Try the two in the corner."

"Okay," Skye said. She took her next shot but missed.

Chad chalked his cue tip and took aim. "Well, you've left a table of good shots. You might as well pull up a chair. This could take a while."

*And I don't mind watching you at all,* Skye thought. She wasn't going anywhere!

Chad's pool skills were in their full glory as he ran the rest of the balls off the table. He racked a second set and continued shooting. "So, girls," he said between shots, "are you excited about the Fourth of July teen program at church?"

"That's right," Morgan answered. "Our first practice is next Friday night. I'd like to be the Statue of Liberty, but I have a slight problem." She chuckled.

Chad took another shot but missed. "Hey, I have an idea. Maybe you could be a perched Statue of Liberty. You could say something like, 'They've given me their tired, their poor, their huddled masses yearning to be free, and I'm tired too.' "

Skye and Morgan howled with laughter.

"Chad, you are one riot." Skye's tone changed as she continued. "I haven't really thought about the program. Do we all have to learn a part or say something? I hope not. I get too frazzled." She took a shot and missed.

Chad started another long run and talked between every shot. "Last Sunday I heard Pastor Newman telling Mrs. Chambers that he wants all the teens to have a part in the program, including the Keystone students. Even though they might not have much to say, at least they'll feel wanted—and needed."

"I know there's going to be a teen choir," Morgan said.

"Well," Skye said smartly, "I'll do anything Pastor Newman wants as long as—"

Chad missed his shot and glanced at Skye. "As long as what?"

"Oh, nothing." She quickly changed the subject. "I'm going to invite Jamie and Les from my class at Madison. Pastor said he'd like to see a whole bunch of visitors the night of the program."

Morgan spoke over her exploding game. "I overheard Mrs. C. telling Pastor that she's bringing all the Maranatha clients to the program. Looks like we'll have a packed house."

Skye took her shot and made a ball in a side pocket. "Wow, a full church! And we only have a month to practice." She shot again but missed.

Chad ran off the remaining balls and glanced at his watch. "I guess we should head upstairs to Pizza World. And I am *definitely* ready." He returned his stick to the mount. "No reason to be frazzled, girls. The Lord will help us with the program as long as we practice, practice, practice."

"Are you inviting anyone, Chad?" Skye turned and put her stick away.

"Yeah, I think I'm going to ask Hannah and her two friends."

"WHAT?" Skye spun around and glared at Chad as if he *were* Hannah. She raked her fingers through her hair, and for the first time in her life, threw a vicious scowl in Chad's direction. "You can't be serious! Since when do you know her?"

Chad recoiled as though a rattlesnake had just struck. "Whoa! What's the matter? We're just friends— distant friends, that's all. Last year we had two classes together. I'd really like to see her get to know God better. Wouldn't you?"

"Well, *I* sure would." Morgan shut down her computer and motored toward the door. The dogs followed close behind. "That girl needs something, and it isn't more money or more snooty friends."

"That's a good point," Chad said as he covered the pool table with a plastic cloth. "Maybe God can do something for her that no one else has been able to do."

"I'll see you guys upstairs." Morgan left the basement and headed up a ramp at the side of the house.

Skye's scowl never left Chad. The hair on the back of her neck prickled, and her insides churned like grasshoppers in a blender. *Chad with Hannah?*

But Chad wasn't Skye's boyfriend, nor could he be until they were much older. Still, the thought made her sicker by the second. *Why should I care?*

Nonetheless, Skye's resentment grew until suddenly, her eyes watered and her throat burned with jealous fire.

"Skye, would you—"

"Oh, never mind!" Skye snapped. She turned her back to Chad, wiped the tears from her eyes, and took off, storming up the stairs.

"What's the matter?" she heard Chad say as she left him all alone in the basement. "Women! Go figure."

"He is *so* stupid!" Skye said under her breath and slammed the game room door.

## chapter seven

O kay, kids! As soon as our stagehands are finished, I'll explain what we'll do next and give out some more parts!"

Pastor Newman, reading glasses perched on the end of his nose, studied a clipboard intently. He stood before the Youth for Truth teenagers packed into the front two center pews in the Community Bible Church. Mr. and Mrs. Chambers and another couple were busy on the platform moving scenery and props. The first Friday night practice for the Fourth of July program had already gone on for two hours, and the entire group looked like they hadn't slept for three days.

After another grueling afternoon with Joey and his horse, Skye let out a sigh of relief when Joey somehow found himself on the opposite end of her pew. "I am *so* glad tomorrow is Saturday," she whispered to Morgan, who was sitting on the aisle in her wheelchair. "I don't think dynamite could get me out of bed before eight."

"You said it." Morgan rested an elbow on the chair and nestled her cheek against her fist. "I am beat as in capital B-E-A-T. Something tells me we're in for a month of hard work. But I think it'll be a lot of fun too."

Chad leaned forward from the pew behind Skye and whispered, "Girls, girls, never mind the hard work. We'll be glad we did this when it's all over."

Skye studied Pastor Newman as if Chad were not even there. *Hannah Gilbert! Humph!*

On the platform, the four adults finished rearranging plywood and cardboard scenery and props. In the back under an illuminated wooden cross where the youth choir would sing, a set of risers had already been assembled. On the left front stage stood an eight-foot-high bell tower. To its right, the men had placed a series of waist-high panels painted like a country road through thick shrubs and bushes. Adjoined to the panels was a facade of colonial row houses with windows and four wooden doors that swung open.

"All ready, Pastor!" Mr. Chambers said. He and the other adults shuffled off the platform and plopped into a pew in front of the piano.

"Thanks, Tom and crew." Pastor Newman managed a tired smile, glanced at his clipboard again, and spoke to the teens. "Did I tell you that we can thank the staff and kids from Junior Church for making all the scenery? I think they did a nice job. What do you say?"

A tired round of applause with a few weak whistles echoed through the small country church.

"And let me just say that I am pleased with your cooperation too." The exhausted man's hazel eyes slowly swept over the entire group. "You all look as tired as I feel, so we won't be here much longer. Mrs. Chambers needs to get the youth choir organized while I briefly discuss the third scene of the program with those involved." He pulled out several half sheets of paper from his clipboard. "Everyone who doesn't have a speaking part in this third section will be singing in the choir. You may go home after Mrs. Chambers meets with you."

Mrs. Chambers stood and forced out a tired smile. "We'll go down to the choir room, go through the medley once, and come back here to show you where you'll stand on the risers. Then we'll be done."

"All right!" several teens said. A few others eked out faint whistles.

The pastor added, "And while the choir is doing that, I'll meet with those who are in this third part. I've chosen the six of you who need to get your instruments ready for the grand finale the night of the program. You'll be able to do that in the choir room during the fourth scene. At our next practice, we'll go over that scene in detail. I did hand out those parts earlier, didn't I?" With his chubby fingers, he scratched the back of his gray head, then shuffled through the papers on his clipboard.

They all mumbled yes.

"Whew! I knew I had those papers here earlier," he said. "I was beginning to think I'd lost them."

"They say the first thing to go when you're old is your memory!" one teen teased.

"Just so I can remember who I am in the morning." Pastor Newman chuckled too. "Anyway, you kids in the fourth scene should have no problem learning your lines before we practice again next week. We don't have time tonight to run through your parts, but you *can* start learning how to sing the 'American Pride Medley' with Mrs. Chambers."

Joey stuck his hand in the air and waved. "Ooh, Mister Pastor, kin I sing too? I love to sing."

While most of the others took Joey's words in stride, Skye rolled her eyes. "Joey, I have something special for you," Pastor Newman said. "I'd like you to stay here with these kids: Melissa, Bobby, Chad, Morgan, and Skye. You'll be in the third part of the program with them, okay?" He then spoke to the choir members. "Now the rest of you may go with Mrs. Chambers."

The Teen Choir, led by Mrs. Chambers, shuffled out the back.

"I hope we don't have to practice a lot," one tired teen complained.

"We'll run through the medley just once." Mrs. Chambers' voice trailed away. "Then we'll come back up here to see where you'll stand on the risers. That's all."

"Good. I'm beat." Other expressions of fatigue echoed faintly above the chatter as the group plowed through a set of swinging doors.

Chad, Bobby, and Melissa joined Skye, Joey, and Morgan in the front pew.

"Ooh, I get to stay with my girlfriend, Cloud," Joey exclaimed as he squeezed himself tightly against Skye.

"Joey, knock it off!" Skye yelled. Like a shot from a pistol, her words ricocheted off the walls of the large, hollow room.

"Oh, I'm sorry, Cloud." Joey's voice quivered. "I—I didn't mean anything. I'm sorry. Don't be mad at me."

Church or no church, Skye could hardly take one more second of Joey Klingerman. Slumping in the pew, she crossed her legs, folded her arms, and simply stared at nothing. *Just great! Now I have lines to learn for this thing, and I can't even get away from him.* Skye's attention shifted to Pastor Newman. Glancing beyond Joey, she caught the looks of those on the front row, who now were all staring back at her. The room was as quiet as a tomb. Skye's usual cool turned into a lather of sweat as her body cringed and her cheeks glowed with shame.

"Oops!" A poor excuse for an apology squeaked out of Skye's lips. Farther down she slid, almost to the floor, while slapping her hands over her mouth. Her eyes darted over to Mr. Chambers, whose furrowed eyebrows gave one clear message: *Young lady, we'll discuss this at home!*

Pastor Newman made an obvious attempt to help Skye out of her jam. "Now, kids, in this third scene," he said quickly and ruffled the papers on his clipboard, "we're going to reenact Paul Revere's last ride. Bobby, you're going to be in the bell tower. All you have to do is raise two lanterns and yell, 'One if by land, and two if by sea!' and 'The Regulars are out!' "

"Wait a minute," Skye said, scratching her head. "What does 'the Regulars are out' mean? I thought the British were coming."

"A lot of people have that wrong," Chad said.

"That's right," Pastor Newman said. "Paul Revere's ride came before the signing of the Declaration of Independence, at which point the colonists still thought of themselves as 'British.' Revere wouldn't have yelled 'The British are coming' because it would have made absolutely no sense to the people he was trying to warn. What he actually yelled was 'The Regulars are out!' The 'Regulars' were the professional soldiers in the British army."

"Wow," Bobby said, "I never knew that."

"Me neither," the others said.

"You mean all I have to say is 'the Regulars are out'? Cool." With obvious delight, Bobby fidgeted with his glasses. Even his spiked hair seemed to stand up straighter.

"That's all." Pastor Newman handed Bobby a small slip of paper. "You'll need to focus on getting your trumpet ready for the instrumental finale with the choir. I think you're all going to sound great." The pastor's glance roved all over his clipboard again. "Let's see if I got this straight from Mrs. Chambers. Chad, you have a guitar; Melissa a clarinet; Morgan ... let's see ... a flute; and Skye, you play the violin. Is that right?"

While the others said yes, Skye nodded weakly.

"But we only have a month to practice," Melissa said.

Slowly, Skye pushed herself upright and listened more intently.

"Now don't worry," the pastor said. "Mrs. Chambers told me she's simplifying your music scores so that our

American Medley Band—that's you!—will sound great, and without having to kill yourselves with long practices. How does that sound?"

"Cool," Chad said. The others nodded in agreement.

"Ooh," Joey chimed in, "kin I play a inskooment too? I love music."

Skye's negative thoughts had already done enough damage. She simply stared straight ahead.

"Yes, Joey," the pastor said. "Mrs. Chambers is going to teach you how to play the tambourine."

"Ooh!" Joey clapped his hands and asked, "What's a tambaline?"

"We don't have one here, Joey, but Mrs. C. will show you at home," the pastor answered. "I'm sure you'll love it."

Joey clapped again. "Thank you, Mister Pastor. I'll do my best. You'll see."

"I know you will," the pastor said. "And you have another important part in the play too."

"I do?" Joey said.

"Yes, you do. Now, how about if you and Bobby come up on the platform with me? In fact, all of you can come, and I'll show you how this little scene will work. You other four are going to be thrilled with your lines." A fleeting smile flickered across his weary face as he turned.

Morgan motored up a ramp behind the organ, while the others followed the pastor. A petulant Skye trailed behind.

"Why will we be thrilled?" Melissa brushed back her long blonde hair. "What about our lines, Pastor?"

"Well, you're each going to be behind one of those doors." Pastor Newman pointed to the plywood row houses. "Joey's going to ride his horse up to your door and yell, 'The Regulars are out!'"

"The Regulars are out!" Joey yelled and then said, "I get to ride a horsey too?"

"Not a real horse, Joey. You'll have a broomstick horse," Pastor Newman said.

Everyone chuckled, except Skye, her face set in neutral.

"A broomstick horsey?" Joey asked.

Mr. Chambers spoke from the front pew. "Joey, we have that at home too. We'll show you later. Just listen to what Pastor says now."

"Okay, Mr. C.," Joey said. "I'll listen real good."

The pastor turned toward the remaining four in Joey's group. "All you have to do is swing your door open and yell in response to Joey, 'The Regulars are out?' "

"That's it?" Chad laughed. "A piece of cake ... although you better give me my line on paper so I can work all week on memorizing it."

Everyone chuckled except Skye, who folded her arms. *Hannah Gilbert will help you!*

"What are we going to wear?" Morgan asked.

"Oh, that's right. I didn't tell you about that, did I?" Pastor Newman poked his glasses back.

The group shook their heads.

"I've checked with Rent-a-Garb downtown. They have late eighteenth-century outfits for all of you. You guys will have breeches to your knees, long-sleeved white blouses, and vests with gold buttons. The girls will have long, full skirts, aprons, and little white hats called mobcaps. You'll look your part, believe me."

*A dress?* Skye's bad attitude stuck out its ugly head again. *I can hardly wait.*

Pastor Newman directed Bobby to the bell tower. "Now, let's just run through this once or twice, and we'll call it a day. Bobby, up you go into the bell tower. Climb the ladder to the seat secured in the back. Just be careful."

Mr. Chambers hurried to the platform. "I'll make sure he's stable. Come on, Bobby."

Pastor pointed to the row houses. "I think it would be wise to put Morgan at the end house next to the ramp so it's easy for her to get on and off the stage. Next to her is Skye, then Chad, then Melissa."

"You're on!" Chad gave Skye the dimpled smile that usually made her heart melt, but tonight her heart was a lump of ice.

The four teenaged actors shuffled to their stations behind the assigned doors. From behind the facade, Skye did her best to look right through Chad to see what the pastor was doing with Joey.

Pastor Newman touched Joey on the shoulder. "Now, young man, you come over here to the left side of the platform."

Joey followed the pastor. "Okay, whatever you say."

With Joey following, Pastor Newman walked down three steps between the piano and a wall. "We're going to have a chair here for you, Joey. You'll sit here so you'll be hidden from the audience. But at the right time, you'll ride your horse onto the stage and say your line. How about if I just do it once for you, and then you can try it."

"Okay," Joey said again. "I'll do my best."

"I know you will," Pastor said and turned toward the belfry where Bobby had just stationed himself. "All set, Bobby?"

"Yep, all ready," he answered.

Mr. Chambers shouted from behind the tower, "I'm going to stay back here and keep the ladder and prop steady for him. He's as snug as a bug in a high rug!"

Everyone laughed. Skye even managed a giggle.

"Are you four ready?" From behind her door, Skye heard the pastor.

"Ready!" she yelled with Chad, Melissa, and Morgan.

"All right!" Pastor Newman held the reins of a phantom horse. "Now, Joey, watch what I do. Here we go. Bobby, raise both lanterns and say your line! Ready, roll 'em!"

Skye watched as Bobby raised two brass lanterns and yelled, "One if by land, and two if by sea!"

Pastor Newman rode his horse up the three steps and galloped to the foot of the bell tower, looking up at Bobby.

"The Regulars are out!" Bobby shouted.

"The Regulars are out!" Pastor Newman yelled and rode across the platform to the row of houses. He knocked on the first door.

"The Regulars are out!" he shouted again.

Melissa casually swung her door open and said in a singsongy tone, "The Regulars are out?"

"Whoa, Melissa," Pastor Newman said. "And you other three back there, stick your heads out your windows and look here a minute."

The teens did as the pastor asked.

"Kids, remember, this is no picnic that Paul Revere is inviting you to. You are alarmed and scared. You are being called to arms—to fight for America's independence! Let's hear some *oomph* in your voices."

"Okay, Pastor," Melissa said.

"Oomph! Got it," Chad added.

"I know you're all anxious to go home." Pastor Newman glanced at his watch and returned to Joey. "Let's just try it once more, and we'll pick it up again next week."

Skye and her neighbors backed out of their window frames and waited for their cues.

"Now, Joey," Skye heard the pastor say as she waited behind her door, "did you see what I did?"

"Yes, sir, Mister Pastor," Joey said. "I kin do this. You'll see."

"Then let's just try it once, okay?"

"Okay," Joey said.

Pastor Newman shouted across the platform, "Bobby and you four over there, are you ready?"

"Ready!"

"All right, Joey, go ahead," the pastor said, "and remember, after Bobby says 'The Regulars are out!' you yell the same thing, gallop across the platform, and knock on each door. I think it would be best if you wait until the door swings open to say 'The Regulars are out!' Just yell it as loud as you can to the person who's standing there."

"Okay! The Regulars are out!" Joey yelled, his round face beaming.

"That's right. Now here we go," the pastor said. "Roll 'em!"

And Paul Revere rode through Lexington, knocking on every single door without a hitch!

## chapter eight

For weeks leading up to the big event, the American Pride presentation at Community Bible Church was the talk of Snyder County. Newspaper ads and radio announcers encouraged all patriotic citizens to "attend the best show in town."

Skye looked forward to the program almost as much as she did the horse show coming in August. Although Joey was stuck in the middle of her life, she tried to focus on her responsibilities with Mom and Dad Chambers' help. However, despite their advice to take her problems to God, Skye decided to handle things her own way. She tried to ignore Joey and Chad, and she kept her thoughts to herself.

Finally, the Saturday evening for the Fourth of July program arrived, and the Youth for Truth were dressed in their colonial costumes, in their places, and ready to go onstage.

From a crack in the door behind the church organ, Skye peeked out at the auditorium. Her heart pounded like a hammer on an anvil. While the pianist and organist played patriotic preludes, every pew in the little church filled with people, elbow to elbow. Latecomers rushed to claim metal chairs that were being set along the walls. The place buzzed with the chatter of friends and family members who had gathered to help celebrate America's roots. Four ceiling fans were trying their best to cool the excitement that heated the room like an electric charge.

"Wow," Skye whispered. "The church is packed. I hope I don't do something lame."

"Do you see Hannah and her friends?" Chad asked.

"No," Skye snapped back.

"Hmm, that's strange," Chad said. "She told me they'd be here."

*Well, whoop-de-do.* Skye squeezed the door shut. Making a point to ignore Chad, she arranged her mobcap over her tight bun of dark brown hair. Melissa and Morgan also adjusted their caps, then all three girls smoothed the long white aprons that topped their flowing skirts. Chad doubled-checked his vest buttons, stockings, and buckled shoes.

"I can't believe I'm standing here in stockings." Chad's brown eyes flashed. "I never thought I'd wear them for *any* reason. And white ones at that!"

Skye forced out a plastic smile and went back to smoothing her clothes.

Morgan's freckled face beamed pure excitement. "I think these outfits are too cool, although *cool* really isn't the best word. I can't believe they wore all these layers of clothes in the summer."

"I know," Melissa said. "I'm melting."

"Well, I know one thing." Skye grabbed two handfuls of her dress and petticoats. "Riding a horse must have been a real pain. I don't know how those ladies kept their balance with sidesaddles. I would *not* have been a happy camper."

"Welcome, ladies and gentlemen, to American Pride!" Pastor Newman made his booming announcement over the microphone.

Skye glanced at the clock. Seven o'clock sharp.

"We're especially glad to welcome all of you visitors who are with us tonight." The pastor continued, "Please remember to fill out the guest card and place it in the offering plate during our intermission. Now, let's all stand and sing, 'The Star-Spangled Banner,' page eight in the hymnal. That's number eight. All four verses, please."

The instruments began, launching the congregation into a hearty rendition of the national anthem. Pastor Newman then prayed, and the teens began their program. While scenes one and two were presented, Skye and her group stood in the hallway behind the door, growing edgier by the second. They rambled on about nothing and checked the clock every five minutes.

"We should be on soon, shouldn't we?" Melissa nervously smoothed her apron one more time. "It's 7:45."

"Listen," Chad said, and they all stood perfectly still.

"... and I know not what course others may take, but as for me, give me liberty or give me death!" echoed through a microphone, and a round of applause exploded.

"That's good ol' Patrick Henry." Skye glanced at a program printout. "So after the intermission, it's our turn."

"I need a mirror." Melissa fidgeted with the long blonde curls dangling in front of her ears.

"You don't want to go into the restroom where they can see you in your costume, do you?" Chad gestured with his thumb toward the congregation. "Everybody—and I mean everybody—hangs out in the restrooms during intermissions. Are you sure you need to go now? You look cool."

"Yes, I need to go *now*," Melissa said.

On the other side of the wall, a swell of chatter and shuffling told the backstage teens that the intermission had begun.

"I need to check how I look too." Skye fingered her cap. "Hey, I just remembered. We can go downstairs to the Junior Church restroom in the back. Nobody will be down there."

"Let's go," Melissa said. "Morgan, do you want to go with us?"

"No, I'm okay." Morgan giggled. "I don't think anyone will notice if my freckles are out of order."

Skye and Melissa hurried downstairs and returned in five minutes. Back and forth they paced while Chad repeatedly checked his buttons and Morgan readjusted her cap. They glanced at the clock and paced, adjusted their costumes, and paced some more. Skye did her best to ignore Chad.

The piano and organ started playing, and Pastor Newman began, "Ladies and gentlemen, we trust that you've enjoyed our program so far. I am so thankful that God has given us freedom in this great land. Join me now in singing 'America the Beautiful,' page twelve. We'll sing the first and last stanzas. Please stand."

"That's our cue. Let's go!" Skye opened the door and the four went into the sanctuary, up the ramp, and took their places behind the facade of row houses. While the congregation sang, the teens checked out each other's costumes and hair one more time. Skye watched Bobby climb up to his perch while Mr. Chambers held the ladder in place. Her eyes darted to the piano side of the platform. There Mrs. Chambers was seating Joey in a chair against the wall. Calm as a toddler ready for his afternoon nap, he sat holding a broomstick horse between his knees. His red cheeks glowed with a jubilant grin from under a three-cornered hat resting atop his bent ears.

*He does look kind of cool.* Skye was surprised by her own admission.

Skye's gaze shifted out her house window and scanned the congregation. Along the side wall three girls stood, talking and giggling.

58

*Hannah Gilbert and her cohorts,* Skye fumed. *Well, double whoop-de-do!*

When the singing ended, Pastor Newman announced, "Please be seated. And now for scene three!"

As everyone applauded, Mrs. Chambers prodded Joey to stand.

Skye dug her teeth into her bottom lip, stepped closer to her door, and prepared to yank it open on cue. "Here we go," she whispered.

Her side vision caught Chad's thumbs-up sign.

"One if by land, and two if by sea!" Bobby shouted as he raised his two lanterns. "The Regulars are out!"

"The Regulars are out!" Joey yelled then rode across the platform.

*Knock, knock, knock.* He pounded on the first door. Melissa swung it open.

"The Regulars are out!" Joey yelled.

"The Regulars are out?" Melissa responded, slammed her door, and giggled. Chad gave her another thumbs-up.

*Knock, knock, knock!* Joey pounded harder on the second door, and Chad swung it open.

"The Regulars are out!" Joey yelled louder.

"The Regulars are out?" Chad yelled back and slammed his door.

Skye straightened her mobcap one more time and grabbed the doorknob.

*Knock, knock, knock!* Joey pounded on the third door, and Skye swung it open.

Silence.

Time froze as Joey stood there, staring blankly at Skye. Then, with no conscious thought of where he was or why, he blurted out, "Cloud, I love you, and Jesus loves you too!"

Skye's eyes registered a mixture of surprise and fear, and her brain went absolutely numb. She stared at the congregation as a wave of muffled giggles broke the silence. Her glance was drawn back to Hannah and her friends, who were holding their sides and practically rolling in the aisle.

Joey, appearing to regain his focus, yelled at the top of his lungs, "Oh, I almost forgot. The Regulars are out too!" The microphone screeched, and the congregation burst into sidesplitting laughs that seemed to charge down the aisles and up onto the platform, attacking Skye like a swarm of angry bees.

Skye slammed her door and leaned against it, her mind a puddle of mush. Her eyes flooded with tears as she looked at Melissa and Chad, whose blank faces registered only, *What do we do now?*

Morgan strained to get Skye's attention. "Skye! Say your line, or Joey won't know what to do next."

"I don't care *what* he does!" Skye blurted out. Bursting into tears, she bounded off the stage and slipped out the door behind the organ. For a moment, she leaned against the wall and wept as if her life were over. With humiliation hot on her trail, she ran down the long hallway, charged out the back door of the church, and tore into the parking lot packed full of cars.

## chapter nine

S kye looked through an ocean of tears, struggling to focus on the Keystone Stables van at the far end of the lot. The evening sun, still beating down mercilessly, drenched her with a wave of hot, sticky air. She ripped off her mobcap, stuffed it in her apron pocket, and bunched her long flowing skirt into a tight wad. Wiping her eyes, she raced toward the van, weaving in and out of a maze of parked cars. *I have never felt so lame,* her heart cried. *My life is ruined!*

Reaching the van, she grabbed the door handle and pulled hard.

Locked!

Skye's layers of clothing choked her frantic body, forcing sweat to ooze from her forehead and join the waterfall of tears. Adding that to the cloud of embarrassment that hung heavily over her only made Skye angrier. A charge of hot temper shot through her from head to toe. Again, she grabbed the handle and yanked and yanked. Somehow, it just had to yield to her persistent force.

"You stupid door!" she screamed. She flopped against the van window, buried her face in her arms, and started to cry again.

"Skye," Mrs. Chambers said as she gently touched the girl's shoulder.

Skye looked into her foster mother's gentle, blue eyes, fell into her arms, and sobbed uncontrollably.

"I hate him," Skye cried. "I know it's wrong, but I do."

Mrs. Chambers caressed Skye in arms of tender love. Not a word was spoken while Skye wept bitterly.

Finally, Mrs. Chambers said, "Let's talk." Holding her foster daughter at arm's length, she gently brushed the tears from Skye's face. "I think you could use some tissues too."

She unlocked the van, and the two climbed in. Mrs. Chambers idled the engine and turned on the air conditioner. Reaching under the seat, she pulled out a tissue pack and handed it to Skye. "Here, honey," she said softly.

Skye emptied her nose into a handful of tissues. Cool air blew straight into Skye's face, squelching her hot temper along with the van's oppressive heat.

"Mom, w-why do I-I feel like this?" Skye sputtered. "I don't want to, but I can't help it."

"Let me ask you a few questions. Okay?" Mrs. Chambers said.

"Okay." Skye wiped her runny nose.

"Why do you hurt so badly right now?"

Skye cleared out her brain and rehashed the last five horrible minutes of her life. "Because everybody in the whole church laughed at me." She sniffled and wiped her nose again.

"I know that's how you feel, Skye," Mrs. Chambers said, "but let's take a closer look at what just happened. What did *you* do that made everyone laugh at you?"

Skye replayed the whole ugly scene in her mind again. "Uh—well—nothing. I didn't have a chance to do anything."

"Honey, perhaps your feelings about Joey have you thinking amiss."

Silence.

"Now, put yourself in the audience, and tell me who or what everyone laughed at."

Skye's mind moved to the front pew where she could get a good look at Joey knocking on her door.

"Well?" Mrs. Chambers asked softly.

"Well, if they were laughing at Joey, I kind of let him down. I should've just kept going. He probably wouldn't have known the difference anyhow." After a long pause, Skye said, "It—it seems like they weren't laughing at anybody. It must have sounded funny, that's all."

"That's right. Often, things that happen onstage are funny because they come as a total surprise. What Joey said was completely unexpected. The audience wasn't laughing at you *or* Joey. I'm so sorry you were caught off guard. The next time we do a teen program, we'll make sure all of you know how to get through a scene if someone botches his lines."

"But why do I feel the way I do about—about Joey?" Skye looked into Mrs. Chambers' blue eyes, searching for a solution to a problem that seemed to have none. Staring out the windshield, she focused on feelings that weighed her down with a ton of guilt and shame.

"Time for another question. Okay?" Mrs. Chambers offered.

"Okay."

"Why do *you* think you're having problems liking Joey?"

Skye thought for a moment and then answered, "He's just in my space all the time. He's there every time I turn around. I feel like I can't breathe!"

"Most girls would be thrilled with that much attention from a boy," Mrs. Chambers kidded.

Skye glanced at the woman and wrinkled her nose. "Very funny."

"Seriously, what is it about this young man that makes you so angry?"

Like a time machine, Skye's brain flashed scenes of Joey from the first time they met. "I—I think it's because I want to serve the Lord, but Joey gets in the way. He smothers me! He embarrasses me in front of my friends too."

"Ah, now we're getting somewhere." Mrs. Chambers reached over and nudged Skye's shoulder. "When you accepted Christ as your Savior and you became a Christian, did things change in your life?"

"You know they did," Skye admitted.

"And what was the one thing you told me you wanted to do as a Christian?"

"From the beginning to the end, I wanted to give my life to God and do things for him."

"And how does a young lady your age serve God?"

"By going to church—and reading the Bible—and praying. You and Dad always tell us that in family devotions."

"I see. And have you been faithful in serving the Lord that way?"

Skye took another brief trip back in time and made a sour face.

"Skye?"

"But Joey's always there, even in church, breathing down my neck."

"Now that you've mentioned family devotions, I have a few more questions for you. Ready?"

"Ready."

"Last month, what verses in the Bible did you kids decide to memorize?"

Silence.

Finally Skye said, "First John 4:19 to 21."

"And what do those verses say, honey?"

Skye took a deep breath and mumbled, "Something about loving God and loving others."

"Could you be a little more specific?"

Skye sucked in another deep, cool breath and surrendered her stubborn will. "All right; I get it. If you say you love God but hate others, you're full of hot air."

Mrs. Chambers chuckled. "Interesting paraphrase, but I think you have the idea."

"Yeah," Skye admitted. "I get it. But right now it's in my head, not here." She pressed her right palm against her chest. "This Joey thing is so hard."

"Honey, I know it is. Nobody ever said the Christian life is easy. But with God's help, we can do it."

"But how?"

"You know we're always telling you that the Christian life is what you *are* on the inside, not what you *do* on the outside. Do you believe God can change how you feel?"

"I guess so. I hope so." Skye wanted it to be true but wasn't quite sure.

"Tell you what. Let's pray and ask the Lord to help you with your feelings. We'll also ask him to help Joey. God loves him too."

"Okay," Skye agreed. "I'm willing to try anything."

Mrs. Chambers glanced at her watch. "After we pray, we'll go back inside. We still have five minutes before the grand finale. Do you feel up to playing your violin?"

"I must look a mess." Skye fingered her hair and pulled her cap out of the apron pocket.

Mrs. Chambers brushed Skye's face softly. "You look beautiful, honey. You even have natural makeup. Your cheeks are sunset red."

Skye squeezed out a giggle and turned toward Mrs. Chambers. "Thanks, Mom," she said with a big smile. "I think I'll soon feel different about a lot of things, especially Joey."

But in her heart, Skye wasn't so sure.

y the time Skye and Mrs. Chambers went back into the church, Skye had managed to calm herself down. Despite the fact that Joey and his tambourine were in the prep room with the rest of the band, Skye put him, and all the trouble he had caused, on a back burner and concentrated on the task that lay ahead. Determined to get the job done right for God, Skye filed onto the platform with a smile and a prayer.

The grand finale, with Mrs. Chambers directing, was performed almost flawlessly. In harmony with the band and the choir, Skye focused on every note. Only once did her eyes stray from Mrs. Chambers or the music score to the wall in the back of the church.

Like a snoot queen and her royal snoot court, Hannah and her friends sat on their thrones, engrossed in the program.

*There's only one reason she's so into this,* Skye thought. *She wants to see me wipe out again.*

But Skye and the Youth for Truth teens gave Hannah no reason to laugh.

At the last note, the band members stood next to the choir. A standing ovation prompted the teens to line up across the stage and take another bow.

Hannah or no Hannah, Skye had done her best.

And her feelings about Joey?

Skye placed him in the back of her mind, simply glanced at the congregation, and smiled.

As the hot summer days drifted by, the folks at Keystone Stables prepared their horses with grueling workouts for the Snyder County Horse Show. Skye and Champ worked on their obstacle course for the Advanced Trail class and helped Joey and Bucky with their routine. While Morgan practiced barrel racing, Mr. and Mrs. Chambers worked with the other students. Chad continued to help too.

As her fickle heart would have it, Skye forgave and forgot Chad's brief entanglement with Hannah Gilbert. He never mentioned Miss Snoot, and Skye was certainly not going to bring up Hannah's name—to him or anyone else.

And Joey? Although Skye's frustration with him appeared to have peaked at the American Pride program, she still struggled with the boy's unwanted attention. Encouraged by Mrs. Chambers, Skye determined to be more faithful in her daily prayer and Bible time. But as she searched for an answer to her problem, Skye's strong will constantly took over, and she resisted what she knew was right. So, deciding to do things her own way, she continued to brush Joey off like a bug on her shoulder. "Skye, how come you're still going into orbit when Joey's around?" Morgan asked in Skye's bedroom late one night.

"Is it that obvious?" Skye asked.

"Is the grass green?" Morgan shot back and giggled.

Skye leaned against her headboard and folded her legs. "I have tried—and tried—to be cool around him. He just rubs me the wrong way."

"Any chance you've asked God for any help with all of this?" Morgan's tone had a flair of sarcasm mixed with her genuine concern. "I haven't seen you even carrying your Bible to church, let alone reading it here at home."

"I haven't exactly been connecting with God lately," Skye confessed. "I guess that's been obvious too."

"Well, duh," Morgan declared. "How many times have Mr. and Mrs. C. said that we need to connect with God—and often. Somewhere in the Bible it says that our time with him is as important as food to our bodies. We don't like to miss the times we stuff our mouths, but we don't think time alone with God is that cool. I've been there too. Sometimes my quiet time hasn't been that important to me. But, sure as sugar, in a few days I'd crash."

"It seems like I've been crashing all summer," Skye said, then her tired voice struggled to portray excitement. "Do you remember that neat Bible library computer program Mom and Dad gave me for my birthday last year?"

"Yep." Morgan forced out a lazy smile along with a long, hard yawn. "You showed the CD to me right after you got it. It *is* neat."

Skye flopped across her bed and rested her chin on her folded arms. "Mom has challenged me to make a list of different ways to love God, so I decided to do a cross-study of the word *love*. You should see all the Bible verses about that."

Morgan stretched her arms and clapped one hand over her mouth to cover another yawn. "Girl, I'm beat. I've got to go to bed, so tell me quick, what about all those verses?"

"Well, there are zillions of them all through the Bible about loving God and loving others. But I found a verse in Matthew that smacked me right on the nose."

"Go ahead, dump on me." Morgan tried to stifle another yawn.

"It says something like if we're kind to others, especially those we'd rather shrug off, it's the same as loving God. I get a big fat F for that one. I haven't been kind to Joey at all."

Morgan rested her head on her fist. "When someone bugs me, I keep reminding myself that God made that person too. Who am I to be putting that kid down?"

Deep in thought, Skye lay like a lump of clay on her bed.

Morgan giggled. "I smell smoke. Are you thinking again?"

Skye giggled too as she looked into the freckled face of her very best friend. "You know, sometimes you are too awesome."

Morgan's sleepy eyes managed to twinkle at Skye's comment. "Me, awesome? How so?"

"Well, you know how my temper's always getting me into trouble. But since I've met you, I can't remember you ever getting frazzled at anything. You're so calm and cool all the time. Now, that's awesome. And you're not mad at God for letting you sit in that chair the rest of your life. That's double awesome."

"Skye, if you wanted to see a mess, you should have known me a few years ago when I was younger and dumber. I used to be really nasty, but I started learning how to keep my smile in the 'display' mode." A Cheshire grin lit up Morgan's whole face while she drilled her cheek with an index finger.

Skye giggled then fell silent again.

Morgan pivoted her chair toward the door. "If you're done with twenty questions, I'm history. Six o'clock comes too early around here."

"Morgan, do you ever wish that boys would pay more attention to you? I mean, you'll be able to date in a couple of years." Skye sat up and dangled her legs off the edge of the bed.

"Sure." Morgan turned back toward Skye. "I've had lots of crushes on guys at school. I wish they'd see me the same way, but they never seem to look beyond this chair. Mr. and Mrs. C. always say that God has someone out there for me when I'm older, but it's still hard to swallow right now. I need a lot of work in that part of my life. Sometimes it can be real tough."

"Do you want Joey?" Skye chuckled.

"Joey? Well, sure!" Morgan kidded as she headed for the door. "He's one neat kid. If you can give him up, I'm sure we'll hit it off just fine."

## chapter eleven

Finished with their daily barn chores on a sunny Friday evening, Skye and Joey walked along the fenced pasture toward the picnic grove. At the pavilion, Mr. and Mrs. Chambers, Morgan, and the other Keystone students were already greeting the Youth for Truth teens who had just arrived for hours of fun, food, and fellowship.

"Cloud, kin I ride your horsey now?" Like a pesky fly, Joey was at Skye again.

"Not today, okay?" Skye spoke more kindly to the boy than she had in a long time. "Champ and Bucky and the other horses are snacking on their oats in the barn. Then they'll take a nice long snooze. Maybe some other time."

"Oh, okay." Joey was always upbeat. "Maybe I kin ride your horsey tomorrow?"

"Maybe tomorrow," Skye said flatly. *And a big maybe,* she thought as she stepped up her pace. "Right now we're going to have a picnic."

"Ooh, I love picnics," Joey yelled. At the end of the pasture, he started running toward the grove. "Hey, you guys," he yelled louder, "we're gonna have a picnic."

Hurrying across the wooden bridge that spanned the brook, Joey melded into the excited group. The teens, armed with bottles of soda, bags of chips, and salad bowls, all greeted him warmly.

*Good!* Skye let out a long sigh of relief. *That'll get his mind off Champ.*

Although Skye considered her "Joey attitude" much improved over the last few weeks, she still struggled with the idea of Joey riding her horse. And with the show only a week away, Skye had been treating Champ like royalty as they practiced for another blue ribbon. Having anyone else ride her champion Quarter Horse now could really mess him up, she reasoned.

As she crossed the bridge, Skye emptied her own mind of horse thoughts and focused on the evening's fun. Her eyes roamed, looking for one special young man among the group of laughing teens.

Off to one side in his chef's hat and red apron, Mr. Chambers was already flipping burgers on a gas grill that sizzled and smoked.

No Chad.

At the pavilion, Mrs. Chambers was receiving the invasion of side dishes from the guests while Morgan stacked paper plates and napkins.

No Chad.

Skye shifted her eyes to a gazebo nestled under a cluster of pines. Three girls were already seated inside, apparently engrossed in each other's news of the day.

No Chad.

As Skye reached the pavilion, she scanned a small clearing near the gazebo. There Chad, Joey, and two other boys were getting ready to start a game of horseshoes.

*He's here!* Skye lit up with a smile from ear to ear.

Mrs. Chambers whisked by and handed Skye a bag of Styrofoam cups. "Would you please fill these with ice? The ice chest is under the table. I've got to get more serving spoons from the house." Mrs. Chambers glanced back as she hurried toward the bridge. "Oh, and Skye, the wet wipes are down at Morgan's end of the table."

"Okay, Mom." Skye cleaned her hands and tackled the task before her. Opening the chest, she started to scoop ice into the cups and line them in neat rows on the table.

"Hey, Skye." Melissa flashed her pleasant smile as she approached with five other girls. "We're going to try a new kind of soccer. Mr. C. said we could play in the field. We're going to practice kicking the ball between piles of horse manure. Want to be the goalie?" The girls all laughed.

"Too cool." Skye laughed too. "But first, I need to help get stuff ready here. I'll join you when I'm finished."

"Catch you later then," Melissa said, hurrying away with the girls.

Skye turned toward the horseshoe pits where Chad was laughing up a storm. For once, she didn't mind missing out on her friends' idea of fun. *I'd rather just watch him*, she told herself as she scooped more cups of ice.

Like a hub in the center of a spinning wheel, Skye stood amid the happenings of an exciting time. From the girls in the gazebo to the boys playing horseshoes to Melissa and her soccer team, the picnic exploded with fun.

But suddenly Skye found herself in a moment of deep thought as she studied Mr. Chambers busy at the grill, Morgan folding napkins, and Mrs. Chambers rushing into the back of the house. *What a family! All they want to do is help. They're always thinking of others. I just think of me.*

Skye flipped back her long hair and turned again toward Chad. *He is so cool too. He even likes to help Joey! All I've ever wanted to do is get away from the kid.*

"Skye!"

As though miles away, Skye barely heard her name called out. "Huh?"

"What are you doing?" Morgan howled with laughter. "We're not feeding the whole church! Just the youth group. You have half the table covered with cups. You go, girl!"

"Oops." Skye started dumping ice back in the chest. "I guess—"

"Never mind." Morgan giggled. "I can see your brain is focused somewhere else."

"You have no idea," Skye said as she headed toward the open field.

Plates mounded with food, intense horseshoe games, and one repulsive soccer ball later, the teens all gathered at the pavilion before going home. Standing at the head of the long table, Mr. Chambers presented a challenge from the book of First John. The topic just happened to be "Loving God and Loving Others."

With Chad on one side and Joey on the other, Skye listened intently to Mr. Chambers. Studying this very subject of love for weeks, she yearned to know more. When Mr. Chambers finished with a question-and-answer time, Skye was into it 100 percent.

"So, kids," Mr. Chambers said, "we've decided that a good way to show your love for God is by going to church, reading the Bible, and praying. But what else can we do?"

Bobby stuck his hand in the air and punched his glasses back on his nose. "We can shape up at home so our parents don't go bonkers!"

Everyone roared with laughter.

"You should know, Bobby!" Mr. Chambers laughed with everyone again.

"I think it's important to invite other kids to church so they can know the truth about Christ," Chad said sincerely.

*Kids like Hannah Gilbert?* With bent elbows on the table, Skye rested her head between two clenched fists to cover her scowl.

Morgan raised her hand. "We can listen when we're in church and not act lame."

"Good point," Mr. Chambers said. "Anyone else?"

"Ooh, ooh, Mr. Chambers!" Joey waved his hand.

"Yes, Joey."

"We can be nice to everybody, especially to my girl-friend, Cloud." Without even looking, Skye knew Joey was gawking at her with puppy-dog eyes. She felt her face start to redden as she stared at a knot in the table.

Everyone giggled.

"And you *are* nice to everybody." Across the table, Mrs. Chambers tried to direct attention away from Skye. "Joey, that's a very good way to show that you love God."

Skye took a quick glance at Joey, whose jubilant smile glowed, once again inviting her into his world.

Strangely, Skye found herself staring deep into the eyes of this special boy. But unlike before, the heat of shame did not surge through her body like poison. Now, for the first time, she saw Joey Klingerman as just another kid who needed help. Her help.

"That's cool," Skye said. From the depths of her heart, an exuberant smile erupted and splashed across her face.

crystal-clear Saturday in August brought crowds of horse lovers to the Snyder County Fairgrounds for the annual horse show. Around a large, fenced oval, fancy-dressed dudes on glistening horses intermingled with parked trailers. Waiting their turn to ride, dozens of contestants tightened cinch straps on saddles, checked bridles and hooves of their mounts, and primped their own western clothes. Others who had already competed were relaxing on their mounts as they watched the show or were at their trailers untacking and pampering their horses.

Cheering fans packed the grandstand while blaring speakers announced the next event. The aromas of barbecued chicken and funnel cakes intermingled with the smells of sweating horses and fresh manure as a cool breeze whisked across the field.

Sitting on Champ outside the show ring, Skye cheered as Morgan and her dun mare, Blaze, raced around three barrels at lightning speed. Along the fence with Skye stood Mr. and Mrs. Chambers, Chad, Joey, and the other

Keystone Stables students, all in western clothes and all screaming their heads off.

Skye looked sharp in her suede Stetson leveled to her eyebrows with her dark hair drawn back in a tight bun. A leather-fringed vest covered a purple-checkered shirt. A black necktie, cowhide gloves, blue jeans, chaps, and polished black boots made Skye a perfect match for her mount.

Champ's black bridle with purple browband set off a leather-cut black saddle. The poncho roll highlighted his copper coat and silky mane and tail. The Quarter Horse's rippling muscles glistened with a lather of sweat as he stood puffing and nodding his head. On the cheek strap of his bridle hung a blue ribbon.

As she watched Morgan compete, Skye caught a glimpse of a familiar snooty face on the opposite side of the ring. Sitting on a golden Palomino near the fence was Hannah Gilbert in the finest western duds money could buy. Her long blonde curls flowed from under a powder blue Stetson garnished with shiny medallions. *I'm glad she's way over there,* Skye thought, *and she can stay there.*

Morgan cut Blaze around the last barrel, raced out of the ring, and headed toward Keystone's group.

"Twenty seconds flat for Morgan Hendricks!" the loudspeaker announced. "That's good enough for second place!"

A round of applause exploded from the grandstand, followed by another announcement. "Attention! All you special cowpokes out there, the Special-Needs Beginners' Western Pleasure class is coming up in about ten minutes, so get your horses ready. But right now, our next barrel racer is Sam Fowler on Tomahawk, a registered Paint."

Mr. Chambers greeted Morgan and Blaze. Grabbing the bridle, he patted the horse's neck. "That was a darn good ride, Morgan. You cut each barrel clean as a whistle. Nice job."

Mrs. Chambers joined him. "That was a great run, Morgan."

"Thanks," Morgan said. "Blaze was at her best today. I'll be happy with a second." She glanced back at the ring to watch the next racer.

"It seems that lately our favorite colors are red and blue," Skye said to Morgan.

Morgan giggled. "Well, if nothing else, we're patriotic!"

Mr. Chambers turned toward Keystone's horse trailer. "We need to get Joey and Bucky ready for their class."

"I'll stay here with the other students," Mrs. Chambers said.

"I'll be right here watching the other racers." Morgan started to maneuver her horse closer to the fence.

"Mr. C., I'll help you get Bucky ready," Chad said.

Skye backed her horse away from the fence and pivoted him toward the trailer. "I think I'll give Champ the rest of the afternoon off. He deserves it." She patted her horse's neck, slid off his back, and led him next to Mr. Chambers and Chad.

"Joey, come with us," Mr. Chambers said.

"I'm comin', Mr. C.!" Joey ran toward Mr. Chambers.

At the trailer, Mr. Chambers backed Bucky, already saddled, down the trailer ramp. "Chad, get me a hoof pick from the cab, will you?"

Skye tied Champ to a brace on the side of the trailer and loosened the horse's cinch. "You'll be glad to get this tight thing off, won't you, fella?"

Joey stood next to Skye and tickled Champ's chin. "He sure is a pretty horsey, ain't he?"

"He sure is." Skye pointed at the buckskin. "But so is Bucky, and you're soon going to ride him in the show."

"Ooh, I get to do that today?" Joey clapped his hands and giggled.

"Today's the day," Chad said as he handed the pick to Mr. Chambers and grabbed Bucky's bridle.

"Are you and Champ gonna help me, Skye?" Joey asked.

"No. You're going to ride Bucky in the ring the way you've been doing all this week. Remember how you've been practicing on the field at home? You'll do fine."

"Oh, okay," Joey said. "I'll do my best."

"We know you will." Mr. Chambers started to clean Bucky's hooves.

As Skye's glance met Chad's, he winked from under his dark brown Stetson. She turned red-hot and returned to her business with Champ. Her heart did backflips.

"Uh-oh," Mr. Chambers said after he lifted Bucky's right foreleg.

"What's the matter, Mr. C.?" Chad asked then also examined the hoof.

"Look here," Mr. Chambers said. "That thrush did more damage than we thought."

Skye hurried to take a look. Joey followed her. "Dad, we kept after that thrush all summer. What's wrong?"

With the pick Mr. Chambers pried underneath Bucky's frog, and the entire pad lifted up. "His whole frog is rotted. It'll take months for that to grow back, if at all."

"But we cleaned it every day," Chad said.

"And dumped hydrogen peroxide on it too," Skye added.

"It's not your fault," Mr. Chambers said. "The damage was done before we bought him. Whoever owned him before didn't keep after the problem. The infection had already started underneath his frog months ago. I knew it was in bad shape, but I was hoping it would last until the horse show was over."

"Is he sick?" Joey asked.

"He's not really sick," Skye said. "He just has a sore foot."

"Does he need to go to the doctor?" Joey asked.

"No," Mr. Chambers said. "Bucky'll be all right, but without that padding on his hoof, he could go lame. He'll need shoes now to give that hoof support. Chad, take his tack off. Nobody's riding him today."

Joey stood back and watched Chad take the saddle off the buckskin. The longer Joey stared, the redder he got. His eyes filled with tears, and all of a sudden he started sobbing as if there were no tomorrow. "My horsey's sick, and I can't ride him!" He cried and cried.

Mr. Chambers poked his cowboy hat back and ran his fingers down his mustache. "I'm really sorry, Joey. I know you worked real hard to be in the show."

Joey ran to Mr. Chambers, fell into his arms, and wept like a baby. His ten-gallon hat fell to the ground as he buried his face in the man's chest.

Mr. Chambers wrapped his arms around him and patted him on the back. "Don't feel too bad, Joey. You can ride him in the show next year."

"Next year" to Joey Klingerman was like "never." He sobbed uncontrollably.

Skye walked back to Champ and started to undo his cinch. Pulling the leather strap free, she stopped dead in her tracks as Joey's sobbing rang in her ears. Like a sign in bright neon colors, the Scripture verse from Matthew flashed before her mind: *The King will reply, "I tell you the truth, whatever you did for one of the least of these brothers of mine, you did for me."*

Skye stepped in front of Champ and stroked his soft, velvety nose. He nickered and then nodded in seeming approval of the decision she knew she had to make.

"Joey can ride Champ," Skye said.

"What'd you say?" Mr. Chambers said over Joey's wailing.

Skye turned around. "I said Joey can ride Champ in the show."

"Are you sure you want to do that?" Mr. Chambers said.

Distraught, Joey turned toward Skye, wiped his nose on his sleeve, and smiled. "You mean I kin ride your horsey now, Cloud?" At that he just beamed.

"Yes, now," Skye said. "This is something I have to do."

Chad slid the bridle off Bucky's head and patted the horse on the neck. "Wow, Skye, that is too cool. You said you'd never let anyone else ride Champ. Ever."

Skye turned and tightened Champ's cinch. "Look, you guys. Champ can do this. He knows the routine inside and out. He trained Bucky. I need to do this. I *want* to do this."

Joey ran to Skye, spun her around, and gave her a big bear hug. "Oh, thank you, my lovely queen. Thank you."

Instead of pulling away, Skye gave Joey a warm hug back. "Come on. Let's get you on Champ so we can adjust the stirrups. You two should make quite a team."

"But how do I ride him?" Joey wiped his nose again.

Chad picked up Joey's hat and plopped it on the boy's head. "Ride him the same way you were going to ride Bucky. And trust Champ to know exactly what to do."

While Skye held Champ's bridle, Mr. Chambers and Chad helped Joey to mount.

"I kin do this, Cloud," Joey said with a tearful smile. "You'll see."

"I know you can." Skye was already leading Champ away.

As they approached the ring, Mrs. Chambers just happened to turn, and her face lit up with surprise. "What's going on? Where's Bucky? Skye?"

"Bucky's thrush got the best of him," Skye said. "Joey's going to ride Champ."

"Kids, look!" Mrs. Chambers said to the other students. "Joey's going to ride Champ in the horse show."

The students cheered as their Keystone Stables team approached the entrance gate and lined up fifth in a field

81

of six. Skye checked Champ's cinch, bit, and bridle, and Mr. Chambers checked Joey's number "10" on his back and the stirrups one more time.

Chad started hurrying toward the judge's stand. "I'll report to the booth about the change in mounts."

"Now remember, Joey," Skye said, "do the same thing you've been doing with Bucky."

"Okay!" Joey's big, broad smile spread all over his face.

"Let's have a quick prayer," Mr. Chambers said, bowing his head. Skye and Joey bowed their heads too.

"Dear Lord, we pray that you'll bless Joey's efforts. He's done so well learning to ride this summer. We pray for Champ's and Joey's safety. In Jesus' name we pray. Amen."

*Yes, please protect Champ,* Skye prayed silently, *and Joey.*

Just as Mr. Chambers finished, the loudspeaker blared, "Attention, ladies and gentlemen, the Special-Needs Beginners' Western Pleasure class is now starting."

The gate swung outward, and six horse-and-rider teams entered, walking single file along the perimeter of the ring.

"I kin do this!" Joey yelled back as he rode Champ into the ring. "You'll see."

Skye and Mr. Chambers hurried to the edge of the ring and leaned against the fence. Skye took a deep breath and watched every move Joey and Champ made. Chad returned shortly.

"Ladies and gentlemen, walk your horses," the loudspeaker echoed.

As though Joey had ridden Champ all of his life, he maneuvered the horse without a flaw.

"Reverse your mounts," the loudspeaker blared, and Joey did so without mistake.

Around the riders went, walking, trotting, turning, and backing their mounts. At last, they were instructed to dismount and lead their horses around the ring. Joey performed exactly as Skye had taught him.

Skye threw another quick glance across the show ring to where she had seen Hannah before. Miss Snoot was still there. While her horse lazily swished flies, she sat in the saddle like a bored rock. With her arms folded, she sneered, her face twisted as though she were sucking on lemons.

*You are so pathetic!* Skye thought as her attention returned to the ring.

Joey led Champ to the center where he lined up with the five other teams. Joey tugged on his horse's bridle. Like a picture in a magazine, Champ stretched out his legs and arched his neck, displaying the champion Quarter Horse features that he and his bloodline possessed.

Skye's eyes never left the judge as he walked to the booth. In less than a minute, he returned to the ring carrying three ribbons: blue, red, and yellow.

"First place goes to Number 10, Joey Klingerman, and his mount, Champ," the loudspeaker blared as the judge handed Joey a big blue ribbon.

The grandstand erupted with cheers as everyone along the fence joined in.

"They did it!" Skye yelled. "Joey and Champ did it!"

"Way to go, Joey!" Mr. Chambers yelled as the others continued to cheer.

The exit gate swung open, and the field left the ring. Joey led Champ to one of the warmest greetings the Keystone Stables folks had ever given to anyone, man or beast.

Skye patted Joey on the back and took Champ's reins from his hands. "Joey, I'm so proud of you. Look at that! You won a blue ribbon!"

"I promised you I'd do it." Joey's voice bubbled. "Champ is the best horsey in the whole wide world."

"Well, Joey," Mr. Chambers said, "you did a great job. Didn't he, kids?"

"He sure did," Morgan said from Blaze's back. The others agreed.

"You're a real western dude now." Chad wrapped his arm around Joey.

Skye, beaming with pride, noticed a powder blue Stetson making its way toward her and her circle of friends. It couldn't be!

But it was!

It was Hannah Gilbert!

Clenching Champ's reins in her fists, Skye watched Hannah like a hawk.

Hannah pushed her way through the tight-knit group and faced Skye almost eyeball to eyeball. *Maybe she's after Chad,* Skye thought as her face burned with confusion.

Mrs. Chambers looked at Hannah with suspicious eyes. "Kids, what do you say we all go get something to eat?"

"Ooh, I'm as hungry as a bear," Joey said.

"Me too," another student said, and the others agreed.

Hannah raised her hand to gain attention. "I don't mean to crash your party here, but I'd like to say something, and then I'll skedaddle. I'd like you all to hear it."

Skye took a step backward. She felt like crawling under Champ. *Oh, no. She's out for blood.*

"What is it, Hannah?" Mr. Chambers said.

"I just want to say that I've been watching you guys for a long time, especially Skye. Chad's been inviting me to your church, but I thought you all were a bunch of fakes. I thought Skye was the biggest phony of all."

Skye put her hand on Champ's neck, twisting his mane in her fingers. She looked at the ground.

Hannah continued. "But I've noticed how you treat everybody the same. With kindness. And Skye? When you let Joey ride your horse after what happened at the Fourth of July program, I knew you were for real. I'd really like to come to your church. Would you be okay with that?"

Skye looked at Hannah with eyes as big as the medallions on the blue hat. She opened her mouth, but nothing came out.

Mrs. Chambers took one step toward Hannah and reached for the girl's hand. "Of course, Hannah; that'll be more than okay. We'd love to have you, wouldn't we, kids?"

"Sure," Joey said. "We love you, and Jesus loves you too."

The others joined in with their agreement.

"I have to go," Hannah said, hurrying away. "My class is up next. See you all later."

"Later," Morgan said.

Skye was still standing with her mouth open.

"Well," Mr. Chambers said, "how about that?"

Skye looked up into the faces of all her friends. "I can't believe it. She really meant that, didn't she?"

Mrs. Chambers' blue eyes sparkled. "I think she did, honey. Which goes to show, you never know how your actions—or reactions—are going to affect someone else."

"I—I just wanted to do what was right," Skye said. "I never thought my letting Joey ride Champ would matter to anyone but me."

"Cloud, it mattered to me." Joey held up his prize. "Look! I won a blue ribbon."

Skye gave Joey her best smile. "And I'm really glad for you, Joey."

"I've been thinkin' a whole big bunch lately," Joey said. "And do you know what?"

"What?" Mr. Chambers looked both amused and curious.

"Yeah, tell us," one student said.

"Well, Skye's my lovely queen." Joey ambled toward Morgan, reached up, and handed her the blue ribbon. "But Morgan's my new girlfriend! She's the prettiest princess I ever knew."

"It must be the freckles!" Chad said.

Everyone broke into boisterous laughter.

Skye joined her friends in the special moment of fun. Her eyes met Morgan's, whose blushing face portrayed a painful, *I can't believe this!*

Skye glanced at Chad. In heart-fluttering style, he glanced back with his dimpled smile.

Then Skye studied Mr. and Mrs. Chambers, her mom and dad, who had loved her through all the tough times, who had loved her in spite of herself. Their faces beamed with pride, that special pride reserved for parents of special kids.

Skye looked at Joey, now dumping all his affection on Morgan, and her heart filled with a new understanding of a special way to love a boy like Joey Klingerman. Now she realized that God loved Joey and had made him for a purpose. Maybe part of that purpose was for Skye Nicholson to grow in the Lord.

At last, Skye understood. She understood that God also loved her no matter what, and she understood that loving God also meant loving others—no matter what. Thanks to Mom and Dad Chambers, Morgan, Chad, and Joey, she now knew what that meant. She would never be the same.

"Now let's all go get something to eat!" Mr. Chambers captured everyone's attention, and a raucous cheer erupted.

Skye threw her arms around her horse's neck and gave him a kiss on his soft, warm cheek. "That's cool," she said. "Really cool."

# A Letter to my Keystone Stables Fans

**Dear Reader,**

Are you crazy about horses like I am? Are you fortunate enough to have a horse now, or are you dreaming about the day when you will have one of your very own?

I've been crazy about horses ever since I can remember. When I was a child, I lived where I couldn't have a horse. Even if I had lived in the country, my folks didn't have the money to buy me one. So, as I grew up in a small coal town in central Pennsylvania, I dreamed about horses and collected horse pictures and horse models. I drew horse pictures and wrote horse stories, and I read every horse book I could get my hands on.

For Christmas when I was ten, I received a leather-fringed western jacket and a cowgirl hat. Weather permitting, I wore them when I walked to and from school. On the way, I imagined that I was riding a gleaming white steed into a world of mountain trails and forest paths.

Occasionally, during the summer, my mother took me to a riding academy where I rode a horse for one hour at a time. I always rubbed my hands (and hard!) on my mount before we left the ranch. For the rest of the day I tried not to wash my hands so I could smell the horse and remember the great time I had. Of course, I never could sit at the dinner table without Mother first sending me to the faucet to get rid of that "awful stench."

To get my own horse, I had to wait until I grew up, married, and bought a home in the country with enough land for a barn and a pasture. Moon Doggie, my very first horse, was a handsome brown and white pinto Welsh Mountain Pony. Many other equines came to live at our place where, in later years, my husband and I also opened our hearts to foster kids who needed a caring home. Most of the kids loved the horses as much as I did.

Although owning horses and rearing foster kids are now in my past, I fondly remember my favorite steed, who has long since passed from the scene. Rex, part Quarter Horse and part Tennessee Walker, was a 14 ½ hands-high bay. Rex was the kind of horse every kid dreams about. With a smooth walking gait, he gave me a thrilling ride every time I climbed into the saddle. Yet, he was so gentle,

Rex

a young child could sit confidently on his back. Rex loved sugar cubes and nuzzled my pockets to find them. When cleaning his hooves, all I had to do was touch the target leg, and he lifted his hoof into my waiting hands. Rex was my special horse, and although he died at the ripe old age of twenty-five many years ago, I still miss him.

If you have a horse now or just dream about the day when you will, I beg you to do all you can to learn how to treat with tender love and respect one of God's most beautiful creatures. Horses make wonderful pets, but they require much more attention than a dog or a cat. For their loyal devotion to you, they only ask that you love them in return with the proper food, a clean barn, and the best of care.

Although Skye and Joey's story that you just read is fiction, the following pages contain horse facts that any horse lover will enjoy. It is my desire that these pages will help you to either care for your own horse better now or prepare you for that moment when you'll be able to throw your arms around that one special horse of your dreams that you can call your very own.

Happy riding!
Marsha Hubler

# Are You Ready to Own Your First Horse?

The most exciting moment in any horse lover's life is to look into the eyes of a horse she can call her very own. No matter how old you are when you buy your first horse, it's hard to match the thrill of climbing onto his back and taking that first ride on a woodsy trail or dusty road that winds through open fields. A well-trained mount will give you a special friendship and years of pleasure as you learn to work with him and become a confident equestrian team.

But owning a horse involves much more than hopping on his back, racing him into a lather of sweat, and putting him back in his stall until you're ready to ride him again.

If you have your own horse now, you've already realized that caring for a horse takes a great amount of time and money. Besides feeding him twice a day, you must also groom him, clean his stall, "pick" his hooves, and have a farrier (a horseshoe maker and applier) and veterinarian make regular visits.

If you don't own a horse and you are begging your parents to buy one, please realize that you can't keep the horse in your garage and just feed him grass cuttings left over from a mowed lawn. It is a sad fact that too many neglected horses have ended up in rescue shelters after well-meaning families did not know how to properly care for their steeds.

If you feel that you are ready to have your own horse, please take time to answer the following questions. If you say yes to all of them, then you are well on your way to being the proud owner of your very own mount.

1. Do you have the money to purchase:

   - the horse? (A good grade horse can start at $800. Registered breeds can run into the thousands.)
   - a saddle, pad, and bridle, and a winter blanket or raincoat? ($300+ brand new)
   - a hard hat (helmet) and riding boots? ($150+)
   - essentials such as coat and hoof conditioner, bug repellent, electric clipper and grooming kit, saddle soap, First Aid kit, and vitamins? ($150+)

2. Does your family own at least a one-stall shed or barn and at least two acres of grass (enough pasture for one horse) to provide adequate grazing for your horse during warm months? If not, do you have the money to regularly purchase quality oats and alfalfa/timothy hay, and do you have the place to store the hay? Oh, and let's not forget the constant supply of sawdust or straw you need for stall bedding!

3. Are you ready to get up early enough every day to give your horse a bucket of fresh water, feed him a coffee can full of oats and one or two sections of clean dry hay (if you have no pasture), and "muck out" the manure from the barn?

4. Every evening, are you again ready to water and feed your horse, clean the barn, groom him, and pick his hooves?
5. Will you ride him at least twice a week, weather permitting?
6. If the answer to any of the above questions is no, then does your family have the money to purchase a horse and board him at a nearby stable? (Boarding fees can run as high as a car payment. Ask your parents how much that is.)

So, there you have the bare facts about owning and caring for a horse. If you don't have your own horse yet, perhaps you'll do as I did when I was young: I read all the books I could about horses. I analyzed all the facts about the money and care needed to make a horse happy. Sad as it made me feel, I finally realized that I would have to wait until I was much older to assume such a great responsibility. And now years later, I can look back and say, "For the horse's sake, I'm very glad I did wait."

I hope you've made the decision to give your horse the best possible TLC that you can. That might mean improving his care now or waiting until you're older to get a horse of your own. Whatever you and your parents decide, please remember that the result of your efforts should be a happy horse. If that's the case, you will be happy too.

## Let's Go Horse Shopping!

If you are like I was when I was younger, I dreamed of owning the most beautiful horse in the world. My dream horse, with his long-flowing mane and wavy tail dragging on the ground, would arch his neck and prance with only a touch of my hand on his withers or a gentle rub of my boot heel on his barrel. My dream horse was often different colors. Sometimes he was silvery white; other times he was jet black. He was often a pinto blend of the deepest chocolate browns, blacks, and whites. No matter what color he was, he always took me on a perfect ride, responding to my slightest commands.

When I was old enough to be responsible to care for my own steed, I already knew that the horse of my dreams was just that, the horse of my dreams. To own a prancing pure white stallion or a high-stepping coal-black mare, I would have to buy a Lipizzaner, American Saddle Horse, or an Andalusian. But those kinds of horses were either not for sale to a beginner with a tiny barn or they cost so much, I couldn't afford one. I was amazed to discover that there are about 350 different breeds of horses, and I had to look for a horse that was just right for me, possibly even a good grade horse (that means not registered) that was a safe mount. Color really didn't matter as long as the horse was healthy and gave a safe, comfortable ride. (But I'm not sure what my friends might have said if I had a purple horse. That certainly would have been a "horse of a different color!") Then I had to decide if I wanted to ride western or English style. Well, living in central Pennsylvania farm country with oodles of trails and dirt roads, the choice for me was simple: western.

I'm sure if you don't have your own horse yet, you've dreamed and thought a lot about what your first horse will be. Perhaps you've already had a horse, but now you're thinking of buying another one. What kind should you get?

Let's look at some of the breeds that are the most popular for both western and English riders today. We'll briefly trace a few breeds' roots and characteristics while you decide if that kind of horse might be the one for you. Please keep in mind that this information speaks to generalities of the breeds. If given the proper care and training, most any breeds of horses make excellent mounts as well.

## Some Popular Breeds (Based on Body Confirmation)

### The Arabian

Sometimes called "The China Doll of the Horse Kingdom," the Arabian is known as the most beautiful of horse breeds because of its delicate features. Although research indicates Arabians are the world's oldest and purest breed, it is not known whether they originated in Arabia. However, many Bible scholars believe that the first horse that God created in the Garden of Eden must have embodied the strength and beauty that we see in the Arabian horse of today. It is also believed that all other breeds descended from this gorgeous breed that has stamina as well as courage and intelligence.

A purebred Arabian has a height of only 14 or 15 hands, a graceful arch in his neck, and a high carriage in his tail. It is easy to identify one of these horses by examining his head. If you see a small, delicate "dish" face with a broad forehead and tiny muzzle, two ears that point inward and large eyes that are often ringed in black, you are probably looking at an Arabian. The breed comes in all colors, (including dappled and some paint), but if you run your finger against the grain of any pureblood Arabian's coat, you will see an underlying bed of black skin. Perhaps that's why whites are often called "grays."

Generally, Arabians are labeled spirited and skittish, even though they might have been well trained. If you have your heart set on buying an Arabian, make sure you first have the experience to handle a horse that, although he might be loyal, will also want to run with the wind.

### The Morgan

The Morgan Horse, like a Quarter Horse (see below), can explode into a gallop for a short distance. The Morgan, with its short legs, muscles, and fox ears, also looks very much like the Quarter Horse. How can we tell the two breeds apart?

A Morgan is chunkier than a Quarter Horse, especially in his stout neck. His long, wavy tail often flows to the ground. His trot is quick and short and with such great stamina, he can trot all day long.

So where are the Morgan's roots?

The horse breed was named after Justin Morgan, a frail music teacher who lived in Vermont at the turn of the eighteenth century. Instead of receiving cash for a debt owed, Mr. Morgan was given two colts. The smallest one, which he called Figure, was an undersized dark bay with a black mane and tail. Mr. Morgan sold the one colt, but he kept Figure, which he thought was a cross between a Thoroughbred and an Arabian. Over the years, he found the horse to be strong enough to pull logs and fast enough to beat Thoroughbreds in one afternoon and eager to do it all over again the same day!

When Mr. Morgan died, his short but powerful horse was called "Justin Morgan" in honor of his owner. After that, all of Justin Morgan's foals were called Morgans. The first volume of the Morgan Horse Register was published in 1894. Since then, hundreds of thousands of Morgans have been registered.

If you go Morgan hunting, you will find the breed in any combination of blacks, browns, and whites. Don't look for a tall horse because all Morgans are between 14 and 15 hands tall, just right for beginners. If you're fortunate enough to find a well-trained Morgan, he'll give you years of pleasure whether you ask him to gallop down a country trail, pull a wagon, or learn to jump obstacles.

### The Mustang

If you want a taste of America's Wild West from days gone by, then you should treat yourself to the "Wild Horse of America," the Mustang.

This 14–15 hand, stout horse has its roots from Cortez and the Spanish conquistadors from the sixteenth century.

Although the Mustang's name comes from the Spanish word, *mesteno*, which means "a stray or wild grazer," he is most well known as the horse of the Native Americans. Numerous tribes all over the western plains captured horses that had escaped from their Spanish owners and ran wild. The Native Americans immediately claimed the Mustang as a gift from their gods and showed the world that the horse was, and is, easy to train once domesticated.

It didn't take long for the white settlers to discover the versatility of the Mustang. Because of his endurance, this little horse soon became a favorite for the Pony Express, the U.S. cavalry, cattle round-ups, and caravans.

Since the 1970s, the U.S. Bureau of Land Management has stepped in to save the Mustangs from extinction. As a result, herds of Mustangs still roam freely in U.S. western plains today. At different times of the year and in different parts of the country, the Adopt-a-Horse-or-Burro Program allows horse lovers to take a Mustang or burro home for a year and train it to be a reliable mount. After the year, the eligible family can receive a permanent ownership title from the government. As of October 2007, more than 218,000 wild horses and burros have been placed into private care since the adoption program began in 1973.

If you'd like a "different" kind of horse that sometimes has a scrubby look but performs with the fire of the Arab-barb blood, then go shopping for a Mustang. You'll find him in any black, brown, or white combination and with the determination and stamina to become your best equine friend.

### The Quarter Horse

There's no horse lover anywhere in the world who hasn't heard of the American Quarter Horse. In fact, the Quarter Horse is probably the most popular breed in the United States today.

But what exactly is a Quarter Horse? Is he only a quarter of a horse in size, therefore, just a pony? No, this fantastic breed isn't a quarter of anything!

The Quarter Horse originated in American colonial times in Virginia when European settlers bred their stout English workhorses with the Native Americans' Mustangs. The result? A short-legged but muscular equine with a broad head and little "fox" ears, a horse that has great strength and speed.

It didn't take long for the colonists and Native Americans to discover that their new crossbreed was the fastest piece of horseflesh in the world for a quarter of a mile. Thus, the breed was christened the American Quarter Horse and began to flourish. Besides running quick races, it also pulled wagons, canal boats, and plows. When the American West opened up, cowpokes discovered that the Quarter Horse was perfect for herding cattle and to help rope steers. Although it remained a distinct breed for over three hundred years in the U.S., the Quarter Horse was only recognized with its own studbook in 1941.

If you are looking for a reliable mount that has a comfortable trot and smooth gallop, you might want to look at some *seasoned* Quarter Horses. (That means they have been trained properly and are at least five or six years old.) They come in any color or combination of colors. Their temperament is generally friendly, yet determined to get the job done that you ask them to do.

### The Shetland Pony

Many beginning riders incorrectly believe that the smaller the horse, the easier it is to control him. You might be thinking, "I'm tiny, so I need a tiny horse!" But many beginners have found out the hard way that a Shetland Pony is sometimes no piece of cake.

Shetland Ponies originated as far back as the Bronze Age in the Shetland Isles, northeast of mainland Scotland.

Research has found that they are related to the ancient Scandinavian ponies. Shetland Ponies were first used for pulling carts, carrying peat and other items, and plowing farmland. Thousands of Shetlands also worked as "pit ponies," pulling coal carts in British mines in the mid–nineteenth century. The Shetland found its way at the same time to the United States when they were imported to also work in mines.

The American Shetland Pony Club was founded in 1888 as a registry to keep the pedigrees for all the Shetlands that were being imported from Europe at that time.

Shetlands are usually only 10.2 hands or shorter. They have a small head, sometimes with a dished face, big Bambi eyes, and small ears. The original breed has a short, muscular neck, stocky bodies, and short, strong legs. Shetlands can give you a bouncy ride because of their short broad backs and deep girths. These ponies have long thick manes and tails, and in winter climates their coats of any color can grow long and fuzzy.

If you decide you'd like to own a Shetland, spend a great deal of time looking for one that is mild mannered. Because of past years of hard labor, the breed now shows a dogged determination that often translates into stubbornness. So be careful, and don't fall for that sweet, fuzzy face without riding the pony several times before you buy him. You might get a wild, crazy ride from a "shortstuff" mount that you never bargained for!

### The Tennessee Walking Horse

If you buy a Tennessee Walker, get ready for a thrilling ride as smooth as running water!

The Tennessee Walking Horse finds its roots in 1886 in Tennessee, when a Standardbred (a Morgan and Standardbred trotter cross) stallion named Black Allan refused to trot; instead, he chose to amble or "walk" fast. With effortless speed comparable to other horses' trots,

Black Allan's new gait (each hoof hitting the ground at a different time) amazed the horse world. Owners of Thoroughbreds and saddle horses were quick to breed their mares to this delightful new "rocking-horse" stud, and the Tennessee Walker was on its way to becoming one of the most popular breeds in the world. In just a few short years, the Walker became the favorite mount of not only circuit-riding preachers and plantation owners, but ladies riding sidesaddle as well.

Today the Walker, which comes in any black, brown, or white color or combination, is a versatile horse and is comfortable when ridden English or Western. He is usually 15 to 17 hands tall and has a long neck and sloping shoulders. His head is large but refined, and he has small ears. Because he has a short back, his running walk, for which he is known, comes naturally.

If you go shopping for a Tennesee Walker, you will find a horse that is usually mild mannered yet raring to go. Although most walkers are big and you might need a stepstool to climb on one, you will be amazed at how smooth his walk and rocking-horse canter is. In fact, you might have trouble making yourself get off!

## Some Popular Breeds (Based on Body Color)

### The Appaloosa

French cave paintings thousands of years old have "spotted" horses among its subjects, ancient China had labeled their spotted horses as "heavenly," and Persians have called their spotted steeds "sacred." Yet the spotted Appaloosa breed that we know today is believed to have originated in the northwestern Native Americans tribe called the Nez Perce in the seventeenth century.

When colonists expanded the United States territory westward, they found a unique people who lived near the Palouse River (which runs from north central Idaho to the Snake River in southeast Washington State). The

Nez Perce Indian tribe had bred a unique horse—red or blue roans with white spots on the rump. Fascinated, the colonists called the beautiful breed *palousey*, which means "the stream of the green meadows." Gradually, the name changed to *Appaloosa*.

The Nez Perce people lost most of their horses following the end of the Nez Perce War in 1877, and the breed started to decline for several decades. However, a small number of dedicated Appaloosa lovers kept the breed alive. Finally, a breed registry was formed in 1938. The Appaloosa was named the official state horse of Idaho in 1975.

If you decide to buy an Appaloosa, you'll own one of the most popular breeds in the United States today. It is best known as a stock horse used in a number of western riding events, but it's also seen in many other types of equestrian contests as well. So if you would like to ride English or Western, or want to show your horse or ride him on a mountain trail, an Appaloosa could be just the horse for you.

Appaloosas can be any solid base color, but the gorgeous blanket of spots that sometimes cover the entire horse identifies the special breed. Those spotted markings are not the same as pintos or the "dapple grays" and some other horse colors. For a horse to be registered as a pureblood Appaloosa, it also has to have striped hooves, white outer coat (sclera) encircling its brown or blue eyes, and mottled (spotted) skin around the eyes and lips. The Appaloosa is one of the few breeds to have skin mottling, and so this characteristic is a surefire way of identifying a true member of the breed.

In 1983, the Appaloosa Horse Club in America decided to limit the crossbreeding of Appaloosas to only three main confirmation breeds: the Arabian, the American Quarter Horse, and the Thoroughbred. Thus, the Appaloosa color breed also became a true confirmation breed as well.

If you want your neighbors to turn their heads your way when you ride past, then look for a well-trained Appaloosa. Most registered "Apps" are 15 hands or shorter but are full of muscle and loaded with spots. Sometimes, though, it takes several years for an Appaloosa's coat to mature to its full color. So if it's color you're looking for, shop for a seasoned App!

### The Pinto

The American Pinto breed has its origins in the wild Mustang of the western plains. The seventeenth and eighteenth century Native Americans bred color into their "ponies," using them for warhorses and prizing those with the richest colors. When the "Westward Ho" pioneers captured wild Mustangs with flashy colors, they bred them to all different breeds of European stock horses. Thus, the Pinto has emerged as a color breed, which includes all different body shapes and sizes today.

The Pinto Horse Association of America was formed in 1956, although the bloodlines of many Pintos can be traced three or four generations before then. The association doesn't register Appaloosas, draft breeds, or horses with mule roots or characteristics. Today more than 100,000 Pintos are registered throughout the U.S., Canada, Europe, and Asia.

Pintos have a dark background with random patches of white and have two predominant color patterns:

1. Tobiano (Toe-bee-ah'-no) Pintos are white with large spots of brown or black color. Spots can cover much of the head, chest, flank, and rump, often including the tail. Legs are generally white, which makes the horse look like he's white with flowing spots of color. The white usually crosses the center of the back of the horse.

101

2. Overo (O-vair'-o) Pintos are colored horses with jagged white markings that originate on the animal's side or belly and spread toward the neck, tail, legs, and back. The deep, rich browns or blacks appear to frame the white. Thus, Overos often have dark backs and dark legs. Horses with bald or white faces are often Overos. Their splashy white markings on the rest of their body make round, lacy patterns.

Perhaps you've heard the term *paint* and wonder if that kind of horse is the same as a Pinto. Well, amazingly, the two are different breeds! A true Paint horse (registered by the American Paint Horse Association) must be bred from pureblood Paints, Quarter Horses, or Thoroughbreds. The difference in eligibility between the two registries has to do with the bloodlines of the horse, not its color or pattern.

So if you're shopping for a flashy mount and you don't care about a specific body type of horse, then set your sites on a Pinto or Paint. You might just find a well-trained registered or grade horse that has the crazy colors you've been dreaming about for a very long time!

### The Palomino

No other color of horse will turn heads his way than the gorgeous golden Palomino. While the average person thinks the ideal color for a Palomino is like a shiny gold coin, the Palomino breed's registry allows all kinds of coat colors as long as the mane and tail are silvery white. A white blaze can be on the face but can't extend beyond the eyes. The Palomino can also have white stockings, but the white can't extend beyond the knees. Colors of Palominos can range from a deep, dark chocolate to an almost-white cremello. As far as body confirmation, four breeds are strongly represented in crossbreeding with the

Palomino today: the American Saddlebred, Tennessee Walker, Morgan, and Quarter Horse.

No one is sure where the Palomino came from, but it is believed that the horse came from Spain. An old legend says that Isabella, queen of Spain in the late fifteenth century, loved her golden horses so much she sent one stallion and five mares across the Atlantic to start thriving in the New World. Eventually those six horses lived in what is now Texas and New Mexico, where Native Americans captured the horses' offspring and incorporated them into their daily lives. From those six horses came all the Palominos in the United States, which proves how adaptable the breed is in different climates.

Today you can find Palominos all over the world and involved in all kinds of settings from jumping to ranching to rodeos. One of their most popular venues is pleasing crowds in parades, namely the Tournament of Roses Parade in Pasadena, California, every New Year's Day.

Perhaps you've dreamed of owning a horse that you could be proud of whether you are trail riding on a dirt road, showing in a western pleasure class, or strutting to the beat of a band in a parade. If that's the case, then the Palomino is the horse for you!

If you're shopping for the best in bloodlines, look for a horse that has a double registry! With papers that show the proper bloodlines, an Appaloosa Quarter Horse can be double registered. Perhaps you'd like a palomino Morgan or a pinto Tennessee Walker?

## Who Can Ride a Horse?

As you have read this book about Skye, Morgan, and some of the other children with special needs, perhaps you could identify with one in particular. Do you have what society calls a handicap or disability? Do you use a wheelchair? Do you have any friends who are blind or have autism? Do you or your friends with special needs believe that none of you could ever ride a horse?

Although Keystone Stables is a fictitious place, there are real ranches and camps that connect horses with children just like Skye and Morgan, Sooze in book two, Tanya in book three, Jonathan in book four, Katie in book five, Joey in book six, and Wanda in book seven. That special kind of treatment and interaction has a long complicated name called Equine Facilitated Psychotherapy (EFP.)

EFP might include handling and grooming the horse, lunging, riding, or driving a horse-drawn cart. In an EFP program, a licensed mental health professional works together with a certified horse handler. Sometimes one EFP person can have the credentials for both. Whatever the case, the professionals are dedicated to helping both the child and the horse learn to work together as a team.

Children with autism benefit greatly because of therapeutic riding. Sometimes a child who has never been able to speak or "connect" with another person, even a parent, will bond with a horse in such a way that the child learns to relate to other people or starts to talk.

An author friend has told me of some of her family members who've had experience with horses and autistic children. They tell a story about a mute eight-year-old boy who was taking therapeutic treatment. One day as he was riding a well-trained mount that knew just what to do, the horse stopped for no reason and refused to budge. The leader said, "Walk on" and pulled on the halter, but the horse wouldn't move. The sidewalkers (people who help the child balance in the saddle) all did the same thing with the same result. Finally, the little boy who was still sitting on the horse shouted, "Walk on, Horsie!" The horse immediately obeyed.

So the good news for some horse-loving children who have serious health issues is that they might be able to work with horses. Many kids like Morgan, who has cerebral palsy, and blind Katie (book five) actually can learn to ride! That's because all over the world, people who love horses and children have started therapy riding academies to teach children with special needs how to ride and/or care for a horse. Highly trained horses and special equipment like high-backed saddles with Velcro strips on the fenders make it safe for kids with special needs to become skilled equestrians and thus learn to work with their own handicaps as they never have been able to do before!

## A Word about Horse Whispering

If you are constantly reading about horses and know a lot about them, you probably have heard of horse whispering, something that many horse behaviorists do today to train horses. This training process is much different than what the majority of horsemen did several decades ago.

We've all read Wild West stories or seen movies in which the cowpoke "broke" a wild horse by climbing on his back and hanging on while the poor horse bucked until he was so exhausted he could hardly stand. What that type of training did was break the horse's spirit, and the horse learned to obey out of fear. Many "bronco busters" from the past also used whips, ropes, sharp spurs, and painful bits to make the horses respond, which they did only to avoid the pain the trainers caused.

Thankfully, the way many horses become reliable mounts has changed dramatically. Today many horses are trained, not broken. The trainer "communicates" with the horse using herd language. Thus, the horse bonds with his trainer quickly, looks to that person as his herd leader, and is ready to obey every command.

Thanks to Monty Roberts, the "man who listens to horses," and other professional horse whispering trainers like him, most raw or green horses (those that are just learning to respond to tack and a rider) are no longer broken.

Horses are now trained to accept the tack and rider in a short time with proven methods of horse whispering. Usually working in a round pen, the trainer begins by making large movements and noise as a predator would, encouraging the horse to run away. The trainer then gives the horse the choice to flee or bond. Through body language, the trainer asks the horse, "Will you choose me to be your herd leader and follow me?"

Often the horse responds with predictable herd behavior by twitching an ear toward his trainer then by lowering his head and licking to display an element of trust. The trainer mocks the horse's passive body language, turns his back on the horse, and, without eye contact, invites him to come closer. The bonding occurs when the horse chooses to be with the human and walks toward the trainer, thus accepting his leadership and protection.

Horse whispering has become one of the most acceptable, reliable, and humane ways to train horses. Today we have multitudes of rider-and-horse teams that have bonded in such a special way, both the rider and the horse enjoy each other's company. So when you're talking to your friends about horses, always remember to say the horses have been trained, not broken. The word *broken* is part of the horse's past and should remain there forever.

## Bible Verses about Horses

Do you know there are about 150 verses in the Bible that include the word *horse*? It seems to me that if God mentioned horses so many times in the Bible, then he is very fond of one of his most beautiful creatures.

Some special verses about horses in the Bible make any horse lover want to shout. Look at this exciting passage from the book of Revelation that tells us about a wonderful time in the future:

"I saw heaven standing open and there before me was a white horse, whose rider is called Faithful and True. With justice he judges and makes war. His eyes are like blazing fire, and on his head are many crowns. He has a name written on him that no one knows but he himself. He is dressed in a robe dipped in blood, and his name is the Word of God. The armies of heaven were following him riding on white horses and dressed in fine linen, white and clean" (Revelation 19:11–14).

The rider who is faithful and true is the Lord Jesus Christ. The armies of heaven on white horses who follow Jesus are those who have accepted him as their Lord and Savior. I've accepted Christ, so I know that some day I'll get to ride a white horse in heaven. Do you think he will be a Lipizzaner, an Andalusian, or an Arabian? Maybe it will be a special new breed of white horses that God is preparing just for that special time.

Perhaps you never realized that there are horses in heaven. Perhaps you never thought about how you could go to heaven when you die. You can try to be as good as gold, but the Bible says that to go to heaven, you must ask Jesus to forgive your sins. Verses to think about: "For all have sinned and fall short of the glory of God" (Romans 3:23); "For God so loved the world that he gave his one and only son, that whoever believes in him shall not perish but have eternal life (John 3:16); "For everyone who calls on the name of the Lord will be saved" (Romans 10:13).

Do you want to be part of Jesus' cavalry in heaven some day? Have you ever asked Jesus to forgive your sins and make you ready for heaven? If you've never done so, please ask Jesus to save your soul today.

As I'm riding my prancing white steed with his long wavy mane and tail dragging to the ground, I'll be looking for you!

# Glossary of Gaits

**Gait**–A gait is the manner of movement; the way a horse goes.

**There are four natural or major gaits most horses use: walk, trot, canter, and gallop.**

**Walk**–In the walk, the slowest gait, hooves strike the ground in a four-beat order: right hind hoof, right fore (or front) hoof, left hind hoof, left fore hoof.

**Trot**–In the trot, hooves strike the ground in diagonals in a one-two beat: right hind and left forefeet together, left hind and right forefeet together.

**Canter**–The canter is a three-beat gait containing an instant during which all four hooves are off the ground. The foreleg that lands last is called the *lead* leg and seems to point in the direction of the canter.

**Gallop**–The gallop is the fastest gait. If fast enough, it's a four-beat gait, with each hoof landing separately: right hind hoof, left hind hoof just before right fore hoof, left fore hoof.

Other gaits come naturally to certain breeds or are developed through careful breeding.

**Running walk** – This smooth gait comes naturally to the Tennessee walking horse. The horse glides between a walk and a trot.

**Pace** – A two-beat gait, similar to a trot. But instead of legs pairing in diagonals as in the trot, fore and hind legs on one side move together, giving a swaying action.

**Slow gait** – Four beats, but with swaying from side to side and a prancing effect. The slow gait is one of the gaits used by five-gaited saddle horses. Some call this pace the *stepping pace* or *amble*.

**Amble** – A slow, easy gait, much like the pace.

**Rack** – One of the five gaits of the five-gaited American saddle horse, it's a fancy, fast walk. This four-beat gait is faster than the trot and is very hard on the horse.

**Jog** – A jog is a slow trot, sometimes called a *dogtrot*.

**Lope** – A slow, easygoing canter, usually referring to a western gait on a horse ridden with loose reins.

**Fox trot** – An easy gait of short steps in which the horse basically walks in front and trots behind. It's a smooth gait, great for long-distance riding and characteristic of the Missouri fox trotter.

# Parts of a Horse

# The Western Saddle

Horn

Gullet
(underside)

Swell

Cantle

Concho

Seat

Jockey

Rear
Housing

Latigo
Carrier

Skirt

Strings

Fender

Riggin Ring

Stirrup

# Resources for Horse Information Contained in this Book

Henry, Marguerite. *Album of Horses*. Chicago: Rand McNally & Co., 1952.

Henry, Marguerite. *All About Horses*. New York: Random House, 1967.

Jeffery, Laura. *Horses: How to Choose and Care for a Horse*. Berkley Heights, NJ: Enslow Publishers, Inc., 2004.

Roberts, Monty. *The Horses in My Life*. Pomfret, VT: Trafalgar Square Publishers, North, 2004.

Self, Margaret Cabell. *How to Buy the Right Horse*. Omaha, NE: The Farnam Horse Library, 1971.

Simon, Seymour. *Horses*. New York: HarperCollins, 2006.

Sutton, Felix. *Horses of America*. New York: G.P. Putnam's Sons, New York City, 1964.

Ulmer, Mike. *H is for Horse: An Equestrian Alphabet*. Chelsea, MI: Sleeping Bear Press, 2004.

## Online resources

http://www.appaloosayouth.com/index.html
http://www.shetlandminiature.com/kids.asp
http://www.twhbea.com/youth/youthHome.aspx